Death at Eagle Roost

Louise Penfold Mysteries – Large Print
Book 2

Eva Bernhard

EB Press

Books by Eva Bernhard

∾

Louise Penfold Mystery Series

Death at Rosewood Manor – Book 1

Death at Eagle Roost – Book 2

∾

Agnes Taylor Mystery Series

Absent Beauty - Short Read Prequel

Silent Sands – Book 1

Writer's Death – Book 2

Snowbound – A Holiday Mystery – Book 3

Stormy Night – Book 4

ISBN 978-1-997787-05-1 (Large Print Paperback)

ISBN 978-1-997787-06-8 (Large Print Hardcover)

ISBN 978-1-997787-04-4 (eBook)

ISBN 978-1-997787-07-5 (Standard Font Hardcover)

ISBN 978-1-997787-08-2 (Standard Font Paperback)

Editorial Services by Pam Clinton at pccProofreading

Cover design by EB Press with a cover image crafted and evolved with AI models by Open AI, NightCafe, and Canva.

This is a work of fiction. All the names, characters, businesses, institutions, places, events and incidents in this book are either the product of the author's imagination or used in a fictitious manner. Any resemblance to actual persons, living or dead, or actual events is purely coincidental and unintended.

Unless adapted, the character's Bible quotes are from *The Jerusalem Bible*, Reader's Edition, 1968.

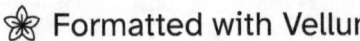 Formatted with Vellum

In loving memory of Nina

Chapter 1

"I've got a job for you. A kind of editorial gig."

In the comfort of her cozy living room, Louise Penfold regarded Sgt. Marpel with some surprise. The young man's rugged face displayed an unaccustomed diffidence, almost unease.

"A job offer?" she echoed, her tone incredulous. "Goodness, that comes unexpectedly." 'From you,' she added silently.

Their relationship was anything but warm. In fact, the odd times she ran into him when visiting his godmother, Nora Norton, at Rosewood Manor, she sensed disapproval. Raymond Marpel certainly never showed gratitude for Nora and her efforts at catching a killer. Back in spring,

1

he'd scolded them for their "reckless interference in a police investigation."

As if divining her thoughts, Raymond Marpel eyed her with a glint of amusement, instantly concealed by bending down to scratch her dog's floppy ears. The pooch scented a dog lover with unerring instinct and had bonded with the sergeant on first sight back in spring. Sprawled at Raymond's feet, Shadow beat his feathery tail on the rug, his black snout buried deeply in the sergeant's sleeve.

Still leaning down, Raymond shot her a rueful glance. "Nothing to do with the cop shop. It's private."

"Oh?" Louise felt a twinge of disappointment.

"It's for my uncle," Raymond said and let go of the dog's ear. He straightened in the armchair, facing Louise squarely.

Shadow's soft brown eyes grew doleful. Resigned to human caprice, the black setter-lab cross laid his moist nose on the young man's foot.

"Not your Uncle Hank--Nora's husband? I mean, he's confined to Rosewood's nursing wing."

Louise didn't want to spell it out. No longer compos mentis, Mr. Norton stood in no need of an editor. The mental and physical incapacity was irreversible at his age.

"Ah, no. It's my paternal uncle. When Uncle Tony mentioned a book project and needing someone to vet the writer, your exceptional editorial and research skills came to mind."

Louise's eyebrows shot up. "You flatter me, Sergeant."

"Not at all." Raymond pointed to the bookshelf behind that housed rows upon rows in evidence of her editorial career. "Your track record speaks for itself, Louise." With a grin that made his strong-boned face almost handsome, he ruffled his sandy hair. "And please call me Raymond. I'm off duty."

"Coming from a trained investigator, that's high praise indeed. Thanks for the compliment, Raymond." She smiled with genuine pleasure, recalling how impressed the sergeant was in spring to learn she researched and edited for a true crime writer he much admired. "Is your uncle writing his memories or something?"

"Er, no. In a nutshell, someone writing a book on the Canadian adult entertainment industry approached my uncle about including his success story." The sergeant's brows furrowed, and his lips pursed.

'He disapproves,' Louise thought. Still, adult entertainment might mean many things. It need not be disreputable. Her tone even, she said, "So, where do I come in? Presumably, the writer does her or his own research and has an editor for the project."

"I realize that. Uncle Tony wants an independent researcher to verify the man's credentials and run a pre-publication check on whatever he writes about my uncle's enterprise."

When she widened her eyes in polite doubt, he continued, "Look, your name cropped up naturally. It's not the man's police record Uncle wants checked, but his publishing record. The last book you edited for..." Raymond mentioned the name of a high-profile Canadian celebrity, "made such a splash. Everyone talks about it. Uncle knows her and was impressed when I mentioned I knew the researcher behind the book."

"Um, yes, I see." And a tremendous editing job it was to whip the woman's sentimental autobiography into shape, Louise thought wryly.

A worried look crept into Raymond's eyes. "You'd be doing me a favor."

"Don't get me wrong, Raymond. I'm grateful to you for recommending me to your uncle. But if he's worried about libel or misrepresentation, your uncle's legal advisors would be his best bet. Whoever writes the book and merely includes a chapter on your uncle's ventures won't appreciate an outsider butting in. The lawyers will know what can or can't be done."

One company's history could hardly play much of a role in a book covering the entire Canadian industry, she figured. Was Raymond concerned about an unsavory connection coming to light and jeopardizing his own reputation? Quite intriguing.

Raymond's defeated gaze clinched it. "Let me think about it," she said as he drained his coffee.

"No worries, Louise. I knew it was a slim chance with you so busy." His face under control again, he placed the mug on the little table at their side and bent to the dog. "Sorry, bud. Need my foot." His hand cradled Shadow's snout.

The gentleness of the movement tugged at Louise's heart.

As they rose, an imperious meow drew their attention. Shadow scrambled to his feet.

A grin flitted over the sergeant's face. "Ah, Magic," he murmured and walked over to the staircase leading to the loft bedroom.

Halfway down its treads sat Magic, her sleek black coat gleaming in the sun's rays filtering through the window sash.

"Goodness. You remember her name," said Louise, truly impressed. He'd only met her adopted feline once or twice months ago. Strictly speaking, if possession was nine-tenths of the law, the cat had adopted her, Louise admitted. Magic had come with the house--sort of.

"Your companions are very memorable." He stroked the kitty with one finger right at the coin-sized white spot below her chin. Magic purred like a miniature engine.

"Well, I'd better let you get back to your work." His square chin jutted to point across the room at her favorite spot by the window wall, over-looking the treed ravine behind the house. Her open laptop on the small table showed what his unexpected visit had interrupted.

Maybe her glance conveyed her yearning to return to it. Whether during breakfast, a tea break, or work, the soft light filtering through the rich autumn foliage of the magnificent maple trees always suffused her with a sense of peace and well-being.

Freelancing, being her own boss, made for a wonderful life, she thought, as she and Shadow walked Raymond to the front door. Domestic squabbles with a cheat of a husband were history. Visitors she welcomed. But sharing her home only with her beloved pets was heaven. She reveled in the thrill of finally being her own woman at 52.

As she watched the sergeant stride along her tree-shaded driveway to his car, his boots crunching on the gravel, a sudden sense of unease made her spine tingle.

"Fiddlesticks," she said to Shadow, and chuckled at the antiquated expression. Besides, she hadn't accepted the job offer. No cause for worry.

Chapter 2

Picture-perfect fall weather gilded the Ontarian rolling hills landscape on Saturday morning. Ideal for a weekend trip to cottage country on Canadian Thanksgiving, Louise thought as she maneuvered her econo-class hatchback onto a minor road up at Georgian Bay. In the passenger seat next to her, Nora Norton mumbled a sleepy, "Are we there?" but sank again into slumber upon Louise's "Not quite."

In the back, Shadow scrabbled on the blanket covering the folded seats. With their bags behind him, he had just enough room to stretch. "Hang in there, buddy," she murmured softly. A seasoned traveler, he always jumped, literally, at an offer of a car ride. No hardship involved.

She hadn't jumped for joy at Nora's invitation to spend the Thanksgiving weekend with friends that Louise had never met. With her laptop's file folders crammed full of editorial work in progress, Louise had planned a quiet weekend at home, sweetened only by autumn hikes in Shadow's company.

Not one to say 'no' easily, Louise had hesitated. Still, Nora's persuasion won the day. It made sense, too. Louise could put in a few hours on her laptop anywhere. And at 70, Nora didn't relish a solo two-hour drive from Cascade on the outskirts of the Greater Toronto Area that might well turn into three hours with the GTA exodus on a glorious holiday weekend. Or that's what Nora had claimed.

Louise smiled wryly at her snoozing passenger. An accomplished amateur actress before Hank swept her off her feet, as Nora put it, one could never be quite sure when this genteel, petite lady put on an act.

Not an adventurous person by nature, Louise amazed herself by falling in with Nora's plan, knowing nothing about the people they were to stay with. There simply hadn't been time in her busy schedule to visit Nora at Rosewood to learn more than a name and their general destination given in a phone call. She'd hoped to find out on the drive. But her passenger dozed off after Louise had programmed the car's GPS.

A glance at the screen showed a switch to a minor road. No street view was available on Google when she checked their destination on her phone upon leaving. Just a gravel road ending at the bay, according to the terrain map. They'd left the main highway with its stunning bay views behind a while ago. At first, the minor road afforded beautiful pastoral scenes of traditional farmsteads, their luscious lawns speckled with golden leaves. Humble cottages rubbed shoulders with upmarket vacation homes.

Farther along the narrowing road, signs of habitation decreased. Trees crowded in. Soon, only the occasional hidden driveway spoke of human presence. Yet, the glorious fall colors against a deep blue sky had Louise gasp in aesthetic pleasure. Her window slightly open, she breathed in the leaf scent warmed by the morning sun.

Their next turn, indicated by the almost muted GPS, caught her unawares. She slowed the car a little abruptly, causing Shadow to scramble to his feet.

"Are we there?" Repeated her passenger, sitting up with a start.

"Sorry, Nora. I didn't mean to wake you. I almost missed our turn. Won't take long now," Louise said soothingly.

"I wasn't sleeping, was I?"

Louise laughed at the surprised tone and understatement. Five minutes after their departure from Cascade, Nora had succumbed to Morpheus. "Just a wee bit. Afraid you missed a glorious drive."

Apparently struggling to shake off sleepiness, Nora wriggled upright. "Where are we?" she asked, sounding worried.

"On the last leg of our journey––shoot!" Louise's attention swerved to a yellow road sign warning of the change of pavement to gravel. She slowed the car to a crawl to avoid sudden bumps on the washboard gravel road.

"I'd no idea the place was that secluded," she said with a quick glance at Nora.

"Nor did I. People say cottage country is crowded now," said Nora.

"Oh? Haven't you visited them before?" A possibility Louise hadn't considered.

"Not for the past 15 years or so. Not since Natalie died." Sorrow tinged the older woman's voice. "The accident was not far from here. That's when Raymond came to live with us."

Louise's foot hit the brake of its own accord.

"Why are we stopping, dear?" asked Nora.

Louise's fingers pressed the four-way hazard button. She swiveled in the driver's seat to face Nora. The excited clicking of the flashing lights underlined her words. "What do you mean? Is this place connected with Raymond?"

Mrs. Norton eyed her with apparent puzzlement. "Not anymore," she said slowly. "Antonio took it all. But Louise, don't you remember? I told you Raymond came to live with us after his parents' *accident*."

The emphasis on the last word had Louise's antenna twitch. Still, first things first. "Who are those people we are visiting?" she asked, her face stony.

"I told you on the phone. My friend Babette invited me for the weekend and said to bring a companion. She knows dear Hank can't travel anymore. Or do anything." The sadness was palpable.

"And who is Babette?"

"Why, Antonio's wife. Raymond's aunt, strictly speaking. But she is so much younger than Antonio. She always insisted Raymond call her by first name only."

Louise's hackles rose. "Do I get this right? We're staying at the house of Raymond's uncle Tony this weekend?"

"Yes, dear. It's their summer residence. Is that a problem? Do you mind?" asked Nora, sounding anxious.

"As a matter of fact, I do. I feel tricked." The extent of the hurt amazed Louise and seemed to astound Nora.

"But why? I grant you, Antonio is sometimes tricky to deal with. Babette is a dear. You'll like her. She always talks about her Pomeranian and just adores dogs." Swiveling in her seat, Nora addressed Shadow, who pushed his nose between the seats to lick the offered hand. "She'll love you to pieces, precious." Her twittering laugh made Shadow thump his tail.

With a sigh, Louise realized, either Mrs. Norton did not get her point, or she was putting on another act. "Could we get back to this Antonio?" she said wearily. "Did you and Raymond cook this up between yourselves? Get me to meet the man without my express consent?"

"Whatever do you mean?" The astonishment seemed genuine.

Patiently, Louise explained, "Raymond visited me earlier this week asking if I'd be interested in doing a job for his Uncle Tony. Vetting some writer or other. I told Raymond I'd think about it. He seemed to take this as the end of the story. Now, I find I'm being lured into the uncle's lair. And out in the boonies, to boot. Don't tell me that's a coincidence."

Nora's attentive, puzzled frown dissolved into a merry chuckle.

"Glad it amuses you," Louise said with unwonted sarcasm.

"But dear, you are mistaken. I didn't have a clue he talked to you." In sober tones, Nora went on,

"It explains Raymond's odd reaction when I told him you'd be coming with me this weekend. 'I hope she knows what she's getting into,' he said and looked strange. You see, Raymond and Antonio don't see eye-to-eye. I was so surprised to hear Raymond will visit, too. Can't recall the last time he's been up to the place. The boy has avoided it since his parents' death."

"I see," said Louise, though that was far from true.

"Do you mind driving on, dear?" Nora sounded almost timid. "They are expecting us for lunch." The fragile hand reached for Louise's sleeve. "You're not mad at me, are you? Honestly, I did not know."

"It's okay." Upon reflection, she added. "Actually, I'm rather curious now. Something about your godson's visit and this strange job offer didn't add up."

"A mystery, you think?" Nora's eyes sparkled.

"Ah, no, I wouldn't go that far. Just a hint of deeper layers."

A cloud seemed to cast a shadow over the older woman's face. "To be honest, I wanted you to meet Antonio, too. And for a reason. You see, it was shabby the way he treated Raymond after the accident. Left the poor boy penniless. Hank didn't agree. He told me it was all above board and Antonio was within his rights. A buy-sell agreement between Antonio and Franco, Raymond's dad. The brothers founded the business together back in the early 80s."

"Sounds like a shotgun agreement," Louise said and put the car in gear. "Shabby perhaps, but not illegal to cut out the son if the father tied all he had to such an agreement."

"Keep your eyes open while we're there." Nora nodded at her own words. "There was more to that accident than meets the eye."

"Oh, come on, Nora. You just love mysteries, and noir at that." Louise smiled, remembering her first visit to Rosewood Manor as a volunteer reader to Mrs. Norton. Nora had whipped out a Raymond Chandler novel to replace the romance, acting as a decoy.

"Mark my words," said the older woman.

Louise kept her eyes on the potholed road that had narrowed into a lane, overhung by scraggly spruce trees. Gray-black rocks, partially covered in moss and ferns, lined their path so closely, Louise could spot mushrooms peeking through the greenish-brown cover.

Past yet another bend, the vista changed dramatically. A hundred yards ahead of them, the bay beckoned emerald green, shading into deep blue.

"Finally." Louise sighed, now feeling the weariness of a long drive. She smiled at Shadow in the rearview mirror. "You'll get a breather in a moment."

"He's an amazingly good dog," said Nora, leaning over to scratch the nose that wriggled closer.

A moment later, Louise pulled the car into a graveled clearing by the shore, next to the vehicles already parked there.

"But where is the house?" Louise asked, glancing around. No driveway or path in sight. A wooden dock bathed in sunshine lay ahead.

"They'll send someone over to get us," Nora said. "I said we'd be here around 11:30." She reached into the pocket of her hunter-green jacket and stabbed her phone with a lacquered fingernail.

"You made excellent time, Louise. We're a few minutes early."

"But where is this place?" Louise cleared her throat, fearing she sounded frazzled.

They both alighted from the car, and she let Shadow out on an extended leash to do his business.

"You can't see it yet. It's past that rocky outcrop over there."

As Nora pointed to a sharp rock formation, a launch-type boat tuckered around it and toward the dock. Its blue and white coat shimmered in the sun-streaked water. The pilot waved his cap in greeting as he cut the engine and docked in a much-practiced elegant curve.

Around 30, Louise figured when they walked closer. Raymond's age. The young man didn't look like a gofer. His stylish tan pants, powder-blue shirt, leather boat shoes, and self-assured posture signaled a higher position in the household.

He placed one hand on a post and vaulted onto the dock. Approaching them, his fingers stroked back the sun-streaked, blond hair. He extended his right hand. "Tyler Quak. So pleased to meet...the three of you." He grinned at Shadow, who sat obediently at Louise's heel. Offering his hand to Nora, he said lightly, "You must be Mrs. Norton. Babette's friend. Glad you are joining us for Thanksgiving."

Nora's eyebrows shot up as he spoke. Louise regarded her curiously. Yet, the genteel "How do you do?" gave nothing away.

"Good of you to come out here, Ms. Penfold." Tyler shook hands with Louise. "We're a little off the beaten track. But you'll find Eagle Roost quite comfortable. May I unload your luggage and help you aboard?"

Thanking him, Louise walked him to the hatchback. Together, they stowed the bags in the boat, just large enough to hold them all. Nora, she noticed, had grown unusually quiet.

Once safely ensconced in their seats, with Tyler at the helm in front and Shadow by Louise's feet, she whispered to Nora, "Are you alright? You're not prone to seasickness?"

"A little," Nora whispered back and grabbed Louise's hand. "I'm a landlubber. Always have been, always will be."

"It's a quick trip," Tyler said without turning.

His hearing must be quite acute, Louise figured. Or it was a routine comment he made when ferrying guests.

They rounded the outcrop and an equally rocky island, studded with stunted evergreens, sprang into view, perhaps 200 yards out in the bay. For a moment, Louise wondered why the dock wasn't on that side of the promontory. Then she saw the granite cliff rising from the shore.

As the boat drew close, a sprawling residence emerged, perched high above a mass of tangled trees and brush that clung precariously to inhospitable rock. Centered between the building's two wings, a glass-encased hexagonal cupola, circled by a narrow widow's walk, rose toward the azure sky.

"Goodness," Louise said. "What a fantastic lookout up there."

Tyler turned his head, smiling. "360 view. Spectacular for watching the sunrise and sunsets. Or stargaze. You'll see the full moon tonight." He glanced at the horizon to the west. "Unless it rains."

"Oh? It looks like a cloudless day," Louise said.

"Weather can change rapidly on the Great Lakes. Lake Huron can be fierce even if the bay is sheltered."

Beside her, Nora caught her breath in a gulping intake. Louise felt the surprisingly strong fingers dig into her forearm for just a split second before releasing with a murmured "Sorry."

Something wasn't quite right, she thought, as they coasted to a halt at the island's weathered dock.

Tyler threw a rope loop over the landing post and said with a broad smile, "Welcome to Eagle Roost."

Chapter 3

Tyler helped them onto the dock. Shadow followed in a fluid leap, shaking himself as though wet. A boathouse hugged the shore.

Before grabbing hold of the luggage Tyler handed to her, Louise scanned the lay of the land. From this vantage point, the sprawling building was partially concealed by weather-beaten trees. Next to its central cupola towered ragged Jack pines, reminding Louise of some famous Group of Seven paintings. The cupola rose far loftier above the cedar-shingled roof expanse of the two-storied wings than she'd imagined.

"How on earth do you get supplies up to the house?" she asked, eyeing with trepidation the steep path leading to rock stairs.

The young man laughed. "No Superman muscles involved." He pointed to the rough-hewn boathouse. Now she noticed a wider path on its side. "We use a souped-up golf cart. The trail winds around. You'll be glad to hear we also maintain a footpath to a splendid lookout. Dogs allowed," he grinned at Shadow.

"You had me worried for a moment." Louise smiled, then looked over at Nora, who had meandered to a bench facing the water. "Maybe you could give Mrs. Norton a ride up in the cart? Shadow and I will love a little exercise."

"Definitely––"

Frantic yipping cut off his words. A furball barreled toward them.

"Spitz! No!" called a high feminine voice from above.

A snow-white Pomeranian threw itself at them in complete disregard of Tyler's, "Down, Spitz!"

"Sit," Louise ordered automatically to ensure Shadow remained politely calm. To her surprise, the adorably fluffy Pom stopped dead and sat at attention in front of her. Black button-nose and sparkling black eyes rose to regard her expectantly.

"Well, I be dam––Sorry, I mean, what's the trick?" Tyler grinned at her.

Louise laughed softly, her eyes on Spitz. "My, what a good dog you are," she said, inordinately pleased at her hidden powers.

Nora got up as a woman rushed toward them, calling, "So sorry. She just won't listen."

"Hello, Babs. No harm done," Nora twittered cheerfully. "We love dogs. So good to see you," she added, stretching out her hands in greeting.

To Louise, the lady of the house appeared quite as stylish as Nora. The loose-fitting rust-red linen pants and long-sleeved white shirt accentuated her golden tan and dark hair. In greeting Nora, she'd lifted her oversized sunglasses and revealed startling blue eyes.

"Meet Louise Penfold, Babette. The friend I told you about," Mrs. Norton said. "And this is Shadow."

Turning to Louise, Babette's full lips parted in a broad smile, apparently taking her dog's transferred loyalties in stride.

"So good of you to let me come along for the weekend, " Louise said. "May I give Spitz a treat? No additives. Pure salmon and fruit," she explained in case the dog had allergies.

"She'd love that," Babette said, and crouched to greet the tall setter-lab. "Hi, Shadow. You're a beauty. So well-mannered too." The pooch nuzzled her hair.

"I knew you'd get along famously." Nora watched the instant rapport between her friends with a delighted smile.

"What a lovely place you have, Mrs. Marpel. I hope we're not too much of an imposition," she added when her hostess's wide forehead creased in a frown.

"Call me Babette, please," she said with a quick glance at Nora. "Let's get you settled. The dogs can romp on the beach or the lawn out back."

She waved at Tyler, who advanced slowly on a golf cart. Louise hadn't noticed him leaving.

"Tyler will give you a ride up, Nora, and see to your bags." She regarded Louise covertly. "If you'd rather wait..."

"I'd love to walk up. Shadow and I need to stretch our legs after the drive." Did she look so out of shape? Louise wondered. Life in Cascade and daily walks with Shadow on the hilly trails had done much for her fitness level.

"I'll explain later," whispered Nora beside her and let Tyler lead her to the golf cart.

The climb to the house was indeed strenuous, Louise admitted when Babette repeatedly paused, ostensibly to point to the truly stunning view behind them. In all its blue glory, the bay shimmered below.

Spitz gamboled ahead, only to race back in hopes of Shadow joining her. Though, as Louise found out, the dogs were much of the same age, Shadow at two almost seemed like a wise elderly gent by comparison. Off-leash would be another matter, Louise told her hostess with a chuckle.

As they neared the house, Babette paused, pointing to the broad stone stairs ascending to a wide terrace that spanned the entire length of the building.

"Mind your step. It's dry now, but they get slippery when wet." She waved to Tyler and Nora, who were just rounding the residence from the far side. Tyler stopped the cart at the end of the terrace and assisted Nora.

"I'll bring your luggage to your room in a short while," he said and reversed the cart.

"Thanks, Tyler," Louise called after him. A thumbs-up acknowledged it.

"Such a nice young man," Nora said, gazing searchingly at Babette.

"Oh, he's alright." It sounded offhand to Louise. The tone changed when Babette continued, "I'm so sorry. We've got a full house quite unexpectedly. I hope you won't mind sharing for one night. Lilly readied the largest room for you. It used to be Raymond's when he had kids stay over. Tomorrow night, you'll get your own rooms."

"We'll be very cozy together," Nora assured her.

Though nothing had prepared Louise for sharing a room with Nora, she took it in her stride.

"I'll try not to snore but can't answer for Shadow." Her pooch was known to saw a log or two after a strenuous day of doggy play. "Er. There's no objection to him staying with us, is there?"

"Of course not," Babette said. "Just keep him away from the vicar's wife. As you know, Nora, Wilma is a little fastidious." She ushered them to a hefty front door in antique wood at the center of the building that sprawled at considerable length but pleasingly angled like a flattened V.

The entry fronted the cupola tower, Louise realized with interest. All thought, however, faded as they crossed the flagstone-paved vestibule.

"Oh, my God! Simply stunning," cried Louise. The hexagonal space opened onto a living area and beyond to a glass-studded rear façade. In the distance dazzled the sun-drenched bay.

"I'd quite forgotten how nice it is," Nora said in calm approval.

Spitz shot past them, her shrill yips magnified by the high ceilings.

"Shut up! You stupid mutt!" a man's voice hollered, drowning Babette's ineffectual shushing.

The dog already bounded back, followed by a thickset man in his late sixties. A shock of icy-gray hair brought out his sailor's tan and deep wrinkles. Except for a paunch straining the navy Polo shirt over gray chinos, he appeared trim and fit.

As he strode near, Louise spotted the crocodile on the shirt's pocket and the shrewd, somewhat piercing glance of the man's narrowed eyes. The facial features bore some resemblance to Raymond's, though the man's jaw line had grown fleshier with age.

"That the lady editor?" he demanded of his wife, the tone coarse but authoritative.

"Good morning, Antonio," Mrs. Norton interceded. "Let me introduce my friend, Louise--"

"Where's that godchild of yours?" He wheeled around, glowering at Nora. "I told him to come early. Business to discuss before the festivities." On the last word, his lip curled in distaste.

"Your nephew," Nora said with emphasis, "has a job that takes precedence over leisure commitments. I expect he was held up."

The man snorted derisively and readied for another attack.

Louise stepped forward, offering her hand. "Pleased to meet you, Mr. Marpel. Thank you for--"

"Marpel? I'm no Marpel." His brows met in a thick welt above his nose.

"Oh? I'm sorry." Louise felt confused. "Raymond said paternal uncle. So I--"

"My fool of a brother took his wife's name. Arcadia wasn't good enough for his father-in-law. Stuck-up ass." Antonio almost spat out the words. "Franco ought to have known better. Old family. Pshaw. Not a penny to their name."

The invective left Louise speechless.

"Natalie's father wasn't like that," Nora rushed to the defense.

"Oh, yeah?" the man scoffed. "Known him intimately, have you?"

Appalled, Louise's eyes widened, cringing at the thought of the weekend ahead. What prompted Nora to accept this invitation?

Babette, whose fingers twisted the diamond rings on her opposite hand, smiled in nervous spasms. Timidly, she said, "I'll show you up now. We'll have drinks on the lawn before lunch at one."

"Thank you," Louise said warmly. "You don't mind if I keep Shadow with me? He can be a little shy in new environments."

"Dogs." Though it sounded derisively, Antonio didn't scowl when he eyed Shadow. "Good-looking mutt you've got there. Well-behaved, too." The frown at his wife was easy to interpret. Though Spitz now sat quietly by Louise's side.

"Come out for drinks then," their host said and left them standing.

"Don't mind Antonio," whispered Nora to Louise.

Their hostess ushered them on. "This way. I hope you are okay with a bit of a climb."

They'd entered the hexagonal space of the cupola tower that connected the entrance hall with the living space. Open straight to the rafters of the cupola, a staircase in blond wood wound its way along the walls to a lofty height. Light streamed in from the windows in the outer walls all the way up to the glass-encased pinnacle.

"What a gorgeous space," Louise exclaimed, forgetting her sense of unease about the unpleasant encounter with their host.

"Thank you. The architect won some awards back in his day," Babette said without enthusiasm.

As they ascended slowly, she turned to Louise. "Nora knows my husband sounds gruff at times. I apologize for him."

"No need," Louise assured her. "We all have our off days."

"You are so right," Babette agreed eagerly. "Some business issues cropped up. He'll be all right again soon." Her hand reached to Nora. "Sorry he lashed out at you, Nora. Inexcusable, I know."

Mrs. Norton favored her with a strained smile. Was climbing the stairs too much for her? Louise eyed her friend closely. Still, Nora lived upstairs at Rosewood and rarely took the elevator there.

Passing a window on the outer wall just then, Louise stood agape at the sight. The water must virtually lap at the tower's foundation. Leaning forward, her nose almost touching the glass, she gasped.

"Oh, my God. I didn't realize. It's breathtaking." Literally, she meant. Below the tower on this side was nothing but a sheer rock face into the water below. Off to the right, the property widened and gently sloped to what seemed a stretch of beach. On the left side, rocks stretched farther out into the water.

Neither Babette nor Nora was much interested, and they ascended to the first floor. Louise would have loved to climb all the way to the roof level for a cautious peek, despite her mild acrophobia. What a view it must be from up there. Her stomach took a leap at the thought of stepping out onto the narrow widow's walk with the sheer drop below.

Babette led them to their room at the far end of the wing to the right, saying, "You can also use these stairs." She pointed to the door across from theirs. "So convenient when Shadow's in a rush. The path circles the entire front of the house and gets you to the lookout trail."

This explained their luggage already waiting when they entered the room.

"Will you be all right?" Babette asked, apparently anxious to leave.

Maybe her husband needed soothing, or other guests waited, Louise assumed. Both she and Nora assured their hostess they had all they needed.

"Come down and join us on the patio whenever you are ready," Babette said. "We'll lunch at one." She bent to grab Spitz's collar, who had already taken possession of the room.

Left to take stock of their temporary domain, Louise unrolled Shadow's pillow bed and glanced around. The room was spacious. Twin beds tucked into opposite corners, partially concealed by attractive folding screens decorated with delicate nature scenes, afforded a sense of privacy. A cozy sitting area faced the windows overlooking the bay. Next to it, Louise discovered a bar fridge camouflaged as a cabinet and well-stocked with beverages and water bottles. Atop sat a basket with packaged snacks.

"Like a luxury hotel," she said as Nora reemerged from the en suite bathroom.

"They always lived well." Nora seemed subdued. Her veined hand stroked Shadow's cranium.

"I'll just give him some water before a quick outing to settle him here while we have lunch. Shall I meet you out back, or will you rest awhile?"

"You go right ahead and give this boy a quick run."

A moment later, when Louise returned with Shadow's water bowl and he began slurping noisily, she saw Nora gaze out a window. From across the room, she appeared even tinier against the glass pane and the shimmering expanse of the bay. Her thin fingers clasped a water glass.

"Natalie loved this place," she said as if to herself. "Raymond was happy here, too."

"I can just imagine." Though remembering the sheer drop at the hexagonal tower's rear, Louise feared for any kid roaming free. "Are his wife and the baby coming along for the weekend?"

"Not as far as I know. Clara is at her parents' place for Thanksgiving. The grandparents adore little Nina." Nora smiled wistfully. "I wonder what Antonio meant by talking business with Raymond."

"Maybe the business issues Babette mentioned require Raymond's professional advice," Louise suggested. "Something to do with the writer chap?" She wondered out loud.

"Uh? What makes you think that?"

"Why? I mentioned it on the drive. An author approached Antonio and proposed including an exposé of the Arcadia company in a non-fiction book the man is writing. Antonio apparently needs someone to check the chap's credentials." As Nora's ignorance seemed unfeigned, Raymond and his godmother weren't in league to lure her out here, Louise deduced.

"Where would Raymond's professional advice fit in? Unless the writer is a crook, it's not an RCMP matter. Antonio is smart to rely on your expertise, Louise." A warm smile accompanied the words.

"Nice of you to say so. It sure is a mystery to me." Louise chuckled. "If Antonio seeks protection from libel, a lawyer is his best bet."

"Hm, yes." Nora finished her water and rested the glass on a side table. "There was never a shortage of shrewd lawyers in Antonio's orbit."

A slow smile hovered on the amateur actress's lips. Her eyes sparkled as she prophesied, "Mark my words. If someone is digging up Arcadia's history, even Antonio might find it hard to slam the lid on."

Chapter 4

It was a frazzled Louise who emerged from the woods an hour later. The trail proved so scenic, and the lookout Spitz led them to was so breath-taking, she lingered far longer than planned. Though she'd leashed Shadow, Spitz dashed back and forth in exuberant puppy joy.

Now, the Pomeranian barreled up the stone steps to the house and, yipping shrilly, shot off around the far corner of the wing to the right.

Seconds later, shouts and cries erupted, almost drowning the frantic yipping.

"Oh, dear!" Louise said to her pooch. "Doesn't sound good." Shadow needed no encourage-ment to pull her to the scene of action.

As they cornered the house, mayhem met them in full cry. Spitz's piercing barks rose an octave as Antonio hollered, "Shut up!"

Other voices merged into a chorus, driving the dog into a frenzy.

For a moment, Louise stood panting from the jog up the steep steps. Disheveled as she felt from their ramble, there was no time to make herself presentable. She took a deep breath and plunged to the rescue––mostly of the Pom.

Rounding the corner, the view of the sloping lawn, dropping off sharply toward the water, would have delighted her if it weren't for the melee of people. Antonio still yelled at the dog, while a matronly woman in a tent-like dress gesticulated wildly to ward off the Pomeranian. Tyler lunged at Spitz, and a somewhat clerical-looking man made ineffectual dashes for her collar. The agile canine enjoyed the fabulous doggy play and promptly upset a tray loaded with drinks.

Instead of calling the dog, Babette tried to pacify her husband, only to have her hand brushed off impatiently.

Abruptly, Antonio's wrath switched to a woman coming out onto the patio above the lawn. Unhurriedly, she placed bread baskets on the table laid for lunch and surveyed the upheaval from afar.

"Shut that crazy mutt up inside," Antonio shouted at her.

The white apron tied over a severe gray dress and the thick dark hair pulled back by a black kerchief and tied in an unbecoming low bun marked the woman as domestic staff. At Antonio's shout, her shoulders slumped into a stoop.

"Do you hear me, Lilly?" her employer roared.

The aproned woman's steep frown deepened, and the angular jaw set in as if she were biting back a rejoinder. Half-heartedly, she joined the fray, adding her monotonous voice to the dog calls.

At the renewed hyperactivity, Louise stepped forward with Shadow at heel. Her hand groped for the whistle she always carried on dog rambles. Its piercing shriek instantly brought everyone, including Spitz, to an abrupt halt, like players in a game of Freeze.

Into the momentary lull, Louise called sweetly, "Spitz. Treat time," and rustled the treat bag.

Next to her, Shadow nudged her knee as if to remind her of his voluntary cooperation. "Good dog," she murmured and repeated it emphatically when the white Pom rushed over to land tail-wagging in a sit.

"Bravo," said an ironic voice from the sidelines.

A man she hadn't noticed before leaned at ease against the patio's pergola post, arms crossed. There was something artistic about his vintage shirt in earth tones, carelessly worn over camel linen pants. A three-day stubble and close-clipped hair, silver-streaked at the temples, accentuated his well-shaped skull. Overall, the curated appearance screamed 'writer,' Louise thought as she bent to grab Spitz's collar.

The woman Antonio had called Lilly approached sedately. With a murmured, "Thank you, ma'am," her work-roughened hand reached for the dog.

"It's okay," Louise said. "I'll clip on the other end of the leash and come with you. Need to freshen up."

"Keep those mutts inside while we eat," Antonio called.

"So unhygienic. I cannot bear dogs near food," Louise heard the matronly woman's contralto.

Must be the fussy Wilma Babette had mentioned, Louise figured, and the clerical man her spouse, the vicar.

Their host strode closer, saying, "Lilly can handle the dogs. Come join us for a drink, Louise."

Louise wiped her brow with the back of her hand. "Sorry about the upset. I'll just settle my dog and be with you in a moment." From the corner of her eye, she saw the writer guy watching, amused.

"No fault of yours." Antonio mustered a benign smile. "My wife should train that dog if she insists on keeping it." His eyes assessed Louise. "You've got a commanding way about you. No one would expect it to look at you."

"Well, I take that as a compliment." She felt far from sure it was one.

Babette joined them, as if uncertain of her welcome. "Please let Shadow stay with Spitz. He's such a calm influence."

Louise laughed. "Didn't seem so just now. But, true, they got on famously on our walk. Love at first sight. Purely platonic, of course," she hastened to add.

"Got him fixed, did you?" Antonio patted Shadow's head. "Poor bugger."

Before he could warm to his theme, Louise made her apologies and rushed to the patio door, where a sullen Lilly awaited her stoically. A chuckle from the man leaning against the patio post told her he still played spectator.

On the French doors' threshold, Louise stood agape, though Spitz strained at the unaccustomed leash. Her glimpse earlier from the hexagonal passage hadn't prepared her for the living space's grandeur. Vast and gorgeous came to mind.

The space soared to the timbered rafters. Light streamed in through the glass expanse on the patio side, throwing dazzling patterns onto the opposite wall.

Furnished in contemporary style, color splashes from accent pieces and abstract art relieved the neutral décor. The effect pleased aesthetically in a high-end interior designer way. No one cocooned here with a good book and a mug of tea. In fact, books were conspicuously absent.

Spitz yipped, impatient for freedom. Louise slipped off her walking shoes and noticed Lilly watching her.

The woman's face went blank as their glances connected.

"This way, please." Lilly's tone was just as colorless when she pointed to a door next to the state-of-the-art open-concept kitchen.

"Is it safe to let Spitz off the leash in here?" Louise's chin jerked at the ivory rug in the sitting area. The rest of the space gleamed in hardwood and Italian floor tiles.

The woman shrugged a shoulder. "She has the run of the house."

Freed from constraint, Spitz careened to an interior door. Evidently, home territory. And no wonder, thought Louise, when she followed inside.

Babette's sanctuary, she guessed. Easy chairs, a feminine desk by the window, collections of knick-knacks, and shaded lamps spelled cozy relaxation. A space for curling up with a favorite romance or celebrity gossip, to judge by the lurid colors of mass-market paperbacks crowding a bookshelf and glossies littering side tables.

Spitz dashed from the water bowl to a pink dog bed and sank her pointed teeth into a plush toy, shaking it wildly.

"I'll refill the water and get another bowl," said Lilly. "Would you like me to fetch your dog's own pillow?"

A glance at her pooch sprawled on the rug told Louise he'd already decided. "Thanks, Lilly. Shadow's fine. It's just during lunch." She bent to pat his silky head. "Be a good boy and wait."

He gave a doggy sigh of content, his eyes following her to the door. Louise closed it softly and followed Lilly into the kitchen. Her gaze roved the streamlined ebony cabinetry, interspersed with brushed stainless-steel appliances. An immaculate kitchen. Spotless despite catering to a house full of guests.

She was about to comment when Nora's genteel voice interrupted from the archway. "There you are, Louise. Did you have a nice walk?" Not waiting for a reply, she prattled on, "Raymond will be here soon. We were texting." She tittered merrily.

Texting, Louise knew, delighted Nora. She smiled at the older woman. "I was wondering where you were."

"Lilly?" Nora's attention swerved to the woman at the sink. "Please hold off lunch until my godson arrives."

The woman shut off the water, and her sullen face turned. "That's for Mr. Arcadia to say." Something like satisfaction at thwarting Mrs. Norton's request flittered across the features.

Yet, Louise didn't believe Lilly liked her employer or his curt orders. He evidently reigned in the domestic realm. The woman's strong-boned face would be quite attractive if she'd shed the drab clothes and severe hairstyle. A makeover would bring out the striking hazel eyes. She'd look like... the analogy eluded Louise. An image seen somewhere...

"Come, Louise. I'll speak to Antonio," Nora remarked a little haughtily.

"Um, go ahead, Nora. I'll run up and change. Be with you in a few minutes." Louise pointed to her trousers. "Dog hair."

The French door opened, and Tyler's blond head poked around the frame. "Lunch at one."

"One-fifteen," Nora said firmly. "My godson is delayed."

"Up to the boss, Mrs. Norton." The young man smiled. "He expects punctuality."

Nora's chin jerked up, and her petite figure straightened. "We'll see."

Worried about their host's temper, Louise sidled close to whisper, "Leave Raymond to fight his own battles, Nora. Let's not make a fuss."

Mrs. Norton shot her a glacial glance, but then softened. "You are right, dear. No unpleasantness this weekend."

Louise gently squeezed the silky fabric of Nora's sleeve. "Thanks. See you shortly."

Refreshed after a quick wash and attired in flattering trousers and a stylish top, with her auburn hair brushed to a shine, Louise pronounced herself fit for company as she emerged onto the patio.

A mild breeze rippled the water in the bay beyond the sloping lawn. The air smelled fresh and aromatic with a whiff of fall foliage.

Out on the emerald expanse of the lawn, the guests lounged in comfortable chairs or stood in animated conversation. A pleasing autumn tableau.

Louise's mood rose a notch. Though not a social butterfly by nature, she looked forward to meeting these people.

"Where's the whistle?"

Though spoken low and smooth, the male voice startled Louise enough to swing around.

"You seem rooted to that spot," she countered as the writer-type pushed a shoulder against the pergola post as if reluctant to unfurl.

There was something cat-like in his movement despite the studied, laid-back air. His mildly sardonic expression was habitual, she assumed.

"You're a writer, aren't you?" she said.

His almost toneless laugh matched the expression.

"Don't say you recognize me." One dark eyebrow lifted with a disconcerting flicker of the intelligent, slightly hooded eyes. Lean and sinuous rather than athletic, his masculinity was palpable.

"Er, no," she said, thrown off her track. "Someone mentioned a writer among the guests, and I just assumed..."

"I look the part," he said with a disarming grin that deepened the creases from nostrils to chin and rippled the black and silver stubble.

He stretched out his right hand. A narrow, braided leather band circled his wrist. The hand felt firm and warm when they shook.

"Hector Gambit," he said. "You must be Louise, the in-house editor. Called in to dot my i's. Fond of red ink, are you?"

"I prefer green wherever I can." It sounded sharper than intended. What had Antonio told the man? Was accepting the weekend invitation synonymous with accepting an editorial gig? Time to set Antonio straight. A quick glance showed their host engaged in animated, if perhaps not peaceful, conversation with Tyler Quak at the lawn's far edge to the water.

Gambit, whose gaze had followed hers, re-marked, "Fair enough. I'll mind my dangling modifiers."

"Let them dangle all you like." She smiled. "I'm off duty."

The man intrigued her. Hard to pinpoint his age, but she judged him a good 10 years younger than her 52.

Briskly, she said, "Well, I look forward to hearing more about your books this weekend. Right now, I'd better join the party."

Again, the almost soundless laugh. This time, it lacked any mirth. "My *book*'s in the making. Ghostwriting keeps me afloat." Self-irony tinged with bitterness, it seemed.

"Oh? The *book* is something major, I take it?" Then the adult entertainment WIP was his only work, in progress or otherwise.

"It's important to me."

Spoken simply, it seemed the first earnest thing he'd uttered thus far. His intense gaze bore wit-ness to her assessment.

As if sensing her awareness, his sardonic expression erased the flicker in his gray-green eyes.

"Let me get you a drink," he offered. "You've got a few minutes until the lunch bell."

"Are you serious? A bell?"

"For whom the bell tolls--to quote the immortal Ernest--time will tell."

"On this mildly ominous note," she replied. "A drink, by all means. Dry sherry, if available. Or white wine, please."

Together, they sauntered forth to join the lawn party.

The clerical, bespectacled man came to greet Louise, stooping slightly in a hesitant gait. From the mild facial features, she attributed the impression to absentmindedness rather than diffidence.

"Are the dogs well-accommodated?" he asked, real concern scrunching his kind eyes. "Spitz is not a naughty dog," he added, as though Louise needed convincing. "Playful and full of beans as the young ought to be."

"Goodness, yes. I agree. Spitz and Shadow are fine. They have Babette's lovely den all to themselves with plenty of water and toys," she assured the fellow as Hector went for her drink.

"Splendid." An almost child-like smile illuminated the studious face. "But where are my manners? Dr. Brown. Everyone calls me Vicar." Even his laugh was surprisingly boyish, taking decades off his middle-aged features.

"Louise Penfold." She shook the proffered pale hand. "Pleased to meet you, Vicar."

"Likewise, likewise. A pleasure, I'm sure. You must meet my dear wife." He looked around, somewhat shortsighted, as if he'd momentarily misplaced his sizable spouse.

"Ah, yes. There is Wilma," he said with a eureka glint behind the spectacles.

'Hard to miss,' thought Louise. The matronly Wilma filled a broad rattan armchair. Enthroned between Babette and Nora in much daintier wicker chairs, the woman appeared to hold court. Well-formed calves and surprisingly small feet protruded under the voluminous tent dress.

The vicar hesitated, whispering, "Might we postpone introductions for a moment? I detect a meeting of the Theatrics Foundation is in progress. My dear wife chairs the committee."

"Quite all right." Louise matched his whisper, feeling slightly silly.

"Here's your sherry." Hector Gambit's soft baritone interrupted. He offered her a delicate tulip-shaped glass, half-filled with the amber liquor.

"Thanks, Hector. Will you join us?"

As she'd guessed, he declined. "I'll leave you to make friends with the indubitable Wilma," he whispered as the vicar stepped forward.

"You mean 'indomitable,'" she murmured and regretted it when she earned a look of scorn. "Of course, you know."

"Know what I mean? And mean what I say?" His keen gaze assessed her. "Neither necessarily nor always," he drawled, and spun away.

"Well, then," Louise told the air and made to join the vicar, who waved, half-hidden behind his wife's chair.

It wasn't to be, however, for just at that moment, a brass ship bell rang from the patio.

'At least,' thought Louise, 'we know for whom that one tolls.'

Chapter 5

"Bid the merry bells ring to thine ear," said the vicar as Louise joined the group around Wilma.

"What's that, Vicar?" asked his spouse and heaved herself from the rattan chair's confinement.

"Shakespeare," said Louise with a smile. The indomitable Wilma's somewhat piggy-like eyes narrowed as if wondering if this was an introduction.

"My friend, Louise Penfold." Nora slid in gracefully to Louise's side. "This is Wilma Brown, Louise. The chair of the Theatric Foundation."

From the corner of her eye, Louise noticed Babette growing restless, shooting glances toward the patio.

So did the vicar. He rubbed his hands, saying, "He gives food to every creature."

This was unlikely a reference to their host. From the mischievous flicker in the vicar's mild blue eyes, Louise assumed it to be a biblical rather than culinary remark.

His "Matthew 6:11" proved her right.

"Vicar," boomed his wife. "You're not on the pulpit."

"Yes, dear." The contrite tone didn't match the sparkle in his glance as he offered Louise his arm with a courteous, "May I be so bold?"

Amused, Louise allowed him to lead her to the table.

The alfresco lunch proved a rich array of cold meat, salads, and side dishes. From the head of the table, unmistakably marked by the only armchair at the far end, Antonio surveyed the straggling guests with knotted brows. His sallow complexion showed crimson blotches.

Another tempest brewing? Louise wondered. Thanking the vicar, she made for the opposite end of the long table, where Tyler pulled out a chair for Babette. The suave writer, Hector Gambit, helped Nora to a seat closest to their host. A moment later, he joined Louise at the foot end.

"Vicar. Another armchair, please," ordered Wilma. "You don't want to pick me off the tiles," she added with unexpected humor.

"Coming up," her spouse responded cheerfully, but was prevented from obliging by Tyler's speedier compliance with the lady's wishes.

Just when Louise was marveling at such a rich fare materializing from an immaculate kitchen, she spotted Lilly and a girl emerge from an inconspicuous door in the side wing of the house.

They carried platters piled high with savory pastries. The scent had Louise's mouth water. She hadn't realized how hungry she was.

Though sitting at the foot end, facing their host, wasn't her preference, even if separated by the full length of the table, the only other choice was a chair across from Nora at Antonio's other side.

Tyler hovered behind the chair next to Babette, with Wilma enthroned in an armchair between their hostess and Nora. On Louise's other side, Hector leaned on the backrest of an empty seat, clearly waiting for Louise. The vicar smiled encouragement and, with surprising alacrity, slid onto the chair across from his wife when Louise obligingly sat down.

She'd expected the vicar to offer a prayer. But instead, he offered prosciutto.

Lilly and a rather pretty girl made their way along opposite sides of the table, serving the fragrant pastries.

"I didn't realize you had other staff," Louise said to Tyler. "I should, though, considering the size of this place."

"Amita's a part-time domestic," Tyler said. "She lives down the road. Her family bought a derelict farm and did a fantastic job of fixing it up. They supply our produce when we're up here."

Their glances strayed to the girl, who helped the vicar load his plate. The man clearly had an appetite. Tyler's attention, however, swerved to their host, and his expression soured. As did Louise's when she caught Antonio ogling the girl. A quick glance at Babette showed their hostess feigned oblivion. Yet, color rose, darkening the golden tan as Babette engaged Wilma in conversation.

Attuned to social dynamics, Nora Norton reacted to the changing atmosphere. Louise smiled as her friend's genteel voice floated down the luncheon table. "What a delicious meal. You're so fortunate to have Lilly." Nora's eyes traveled from Babette back to Antonio and on to the young server, now offering pastries to Hector. "And you are doing a fine job, Amita."

"Thank you, ma'am," the girl responded with a sweet smile.

"Domestic staff's way too expensive these days," growled their host. "If the socialists keep hiking up minimum wage..." His hand flapped, dismissing the rest.

"What socialists might that be, sir?" Hector Gambit's face expressed polite interest.

"Socialists. Social democrats. Same difference. Blood suckers, all of them." Their host's cheeks took on a burgundy tint. His voice rose. "How's a man to make money? Social security contributions. A stranglehold on business, I tell you."

"I thought in your line of business you hire your 'entertainers' as independent contractors and let them worry about their own 'security,'" Gambit said, a hint of sarcasm emphasizing key words.

For a moment, Antonio appeared taken aback. Then he hissed like a cobra. "Who told you that?"

Louise watched her neighbor closely. His long, tapered fingers ripped a chunk of baguette to shreds. No emotion colored his words as he replied, "I'm a researcher."

"What's that supposed to mean?" Antonio waved a bread knife before carving a baguette into thin slices with expert precision.

"Fact finding is the..." Hector paused, his eyes following the path of their host's sawtooth knife as it dove into a butter dish. He continued, "It's the bread and butter of non-fiction writers."

The cliché had Louise doubting the quality of Gambit's prose.

Antonio glared down the length of the table. "Don't tell me my employees' contracts are posted on the web."

"Isn't it amazing what you can find on the internet?" twittered Nora. "I just love browsing. Goodness, the things posted about people... So much more interesting than old folks' gossip at Rosewood." Her expressive, fragile hand went to cover the carefully outlined lips in mock astonishment.

"You should know," said Antonio, stuffing a buttered slice into his wide mouth. "Always were a nosy cat," he muttered.

To divert their host's ire from her friend, Louise remarked, "It's indeed astonishing how helpful the internet can be in research if one screens for reliable sources." She shifted in her seat to include Hector. "Do you find AI useful in your work?"

"Eh?" Her neighbor stiffened. His response was disappointingly vague. "Depends, doesn't it?"

Across, Wilma Brown's posture straightened. Thus far, she'd devoted her full attention to partaking of every dish, often bidding the vicar to supply her wants of dainties out of her reach.

Now, her sonorous voice took center stage, announcing, "AI's the death knell of acting."

"They've said that of the pictures." Nora smiled from one to the other. "When the first silent films came out, theaters feared the worst."

"Remember it clearly, don't you?"

Antonio's sarcasm left Nora unaffected. She tittered merrily and leaned in to air-slap his hand playfully.

"Naughty man," she said. "We're much the same age, Tony. What do three years matter at our time in life?"

"Three years matter a lot to some people," Gambit remarked, staring at his empty wineglass. "A hell of a lot if you lose them."

A half-suppressed chortle from Tyler Quak rerouted Louise's attention to her other neighbor. But he had his face under control and gazed at Gambit with a bland expression.

Diagonally behind Tyler, Louise saw Lilly hover in the shade of a window niche. Had the enigmatic woman waited in the wings the entire time?

There was no sign of Amita.

Next to Tyler, Babette toyed with the food on her plate, a pained expression pinching her pampered features. Louise's mind had noted a low ebbing and flowing of conversation, like an undercurrent to the table talk. Now, neither Babette nor Tyler was inclined to chat.

The vicar's amiable voice cut into Louise's reflections. "The lost son returns to the fold. Or is it the errant sheep?" His boyish laugh was lost in a frantic yipping.

A white canine bundle of energy careened along the length of the table, shooting in and out between chair legs.

Wilma shrieked and almost toppled the armchair as she scrambled to her feet.

"Lilly!" hollered Antonio. "Where's that darn woman?"

The vicar beamed as though he hadn't had that much fun in ages.

Beside Louise, Hector leaned close. "Where's your whistle?" He sounded genuinely amused.

"Never whistle at table." Louise grinned at him.

Into the upheaval strode Sergeant Marpel. Plain clothed in casual attire. He appeared much younger in jeans and a T-shirt, Louise thought.

Somehow more informal than any of them, even Hector and Tyler.

Now, he put two fingers into his mouth and issued a piercing whistle.

Like a meteor, the white Pomeranian dashed to heed the summons. Shadow emerged sedately from the French doors that now stood wide open. Both dogs sat facing Raymond expectantly.

"Almost as good as your act," murmured Hector.

"Oh, quite better, considering neither dog is his," Louise said, impressed at the sergeant's canine rapport.

Nora rushed over to embrace her godson, her tiny figure reaching to his chest. He leaned in to kiss the top of her coiffured head.

Shadow gave up on potential treats and trotted over to Louise, his tail wagging in hesitant spurts as if in doubt of his welcome.

"Not your fault," Louise murmured and rubbed his ear. "You'll get another walk later."

"That's a beautiful dog you've got," Gambit said.

From her other side, Tyler bent over to stroke Shadow's head.

"Lilly!" Antonio barked. "Lock up that menace of a dog."

On his feet now, fists clenching the tabletop corners, he leaned forward and glowered at Babette. "If you're incapable of teaching that dog any manners, I'll have it destroyed. Or shoot it myself."

"No!" Babette's cry rang in the air. "If you touch my dog--" her voice broke and, bursting into tears, she sprang up and grabbed the Pomeranian. The pup yelped at being lifted so abruptly. Cradling Spitz in her arms, Babette ran into the house.

Tyler half rose as if to follow, then sank back into his chair. To Louise, it seemed his smoldering glance pierced his boss from afar.

"Monster," muttered Gambit.

"You!" Antonio lumbered over to his nephew, his stocky body swaying from side to side. "Come to my office, boy. We've got to talk."

"Don't call me 'boy.' I'm a mature adult if you haven't noticed." Raymond sounded peevish to

Louise's ears. Quite unlike the sergeant's professional persona she'd encountered in Cascade. Antonio certainly brought out the worst in everyone.

"No, I hadn't noticed." Antonio's sarcasm made Raymond flinch. "Act like a man and you'll get treated like one."

An irate Nora turned on their host like a small tigress. "He's more of a man than––"

Raymond hugged her close. "Don't..." The rest was a murmur lost to others.

His uncle scowled at them. "I want you now." With that, he strode to the French doors. On their threshold, he called over his shoulder, "Gambit. Give Louise that scribbling of yours."

"But, Antonio," cried Louise, feeling railroaded. "We haven't even––"

"Money's no object," he retorted. "Charge whatever you like." With that, he barged into the living room.

"Sorry about that," Raymond said. "I apologize for letting loose the hellhound. Ruined your lunch. Unforgivable."

"Not at all." The vicar's eyes sparkled. "Don't give it another thought."

"I believe your uncle is waiting." Wilma carved a piece of meat and didn't glance up from her plate.

"You'd better go," Nora said. "We'll catch up later."

Raymond kissed his godmother's cheek, waved at Louise, and unhurriedly followed his uncle.

Both Hector and Tyler had observed the young man somewhat furtively, Louise thought. In a writer, such covert interest in drama seemed par for the course.

Yet, what was Tyler Quak's role in this menage? she wondered.

Chapter 6

Non-plussed at Antonio's high-handedness and his shocking rudeness, Louise told Gambit, "Don't feel you must share your writing with me, Hector. I'd no chance to discuss this with Antonio. Never mind agreeing to take on any job for him."

"Er?" The writer's gaze shifted from the French doors to her face without focusing.

"No author appreciates others butting in unasked," Louise said. "I'm sure you have your own editor. If Antonio worries about inaccuracies––"

"I don't." Gambit's snort sounded bitter. "Ghostwriters don't." His glance lingered on her face.

"If Arcadia wants to pay for an editorial assessment, that's fine with me. As long as I get an unabridged copy."

"Still..." Louise hesitated. By now, she was curious to read what he'd come up with.

"I meant it. Assuming you're objective and fair--which by all accounts you are."

Her raised eyebrow deepened his disarming grin. "I Googled you, of course," he went on. "As I'm sure you did me."

"Not yet. I wanted to meet the person and form my own opinion before sifting the net for kernels of truth."

His fingers rubbed the stubble on his chin. "Corporeal presence trumps digital? Don't editors deal in the spirit of the letter?"

"Up to a point. I specialize in fact checking."

That earned her a genuine laugh. A pleasant one, too.

"The most prolific of my clients writes true crime," she explained. "Unraveling facts makes all the difference between a guilty and not guilty verdict."

Again Gambit laughed. Yet without merriment. His eyes became impenetrable, as if their gray shrouded any sparkle of green.

"Justice prevails? We've entered the realm of fairy tales."

"You sound a little cynical." Years of crime research, however, taught her not to take justice for granted.

Gambit stared at the window expanse that reflected the shimmering bay. "Right. I'll pass on my scribbles." He rose, not meeting her glance.

"No rush. I need to speak to Antonio first. We have all weekend."

About to reply, he seemed to change his mind and walked off with a slight wave.

"May I take your plate, ma'am?"

Amita's young voice startled Louise, whose gaze had followed Hector.

"Sorry, Amita," she said. "My mind was wandering. You and Lilly must be terribly busy today."

The girl smiled. "It's not like their large parties. The kitchen here is awesome. Way better than our old farm kitchen."

"It's splendid, isn't it? And wonderfully tidy. My kitchen would be a mess if I catered lunch for eight or ten people."

"Oh, no, ma'am. That one's just for show." Amita clapped a graceful hand over her mouth. "I don't mean 'show off.' It's like––the real work we do in the basement kitchen."

"Ah, that explains it." Louise smiled. "No trace of food odor––so I should have guessed." She had, in fact, when she saw the servers emerge from the side door. It wasn't unusual in Italian households to have a second kitchen in the basement.

"The boss doesn't like the place reeking of food, he says." Amita seemed happy to gossip. She shot a glance at her colleague, clearing the other end of the table.

Nora and Wilma, Louise noticed, had retreated to the comfortable lawn chairs. Tyler must have left earlier. The vicar strolled along the herbaceous border. Like a bee fluttering from flower to flower, he poked his nose into the blossoms he picked.

"Lilly doesn't like all the running up and down with stuff," Amita said, dawdling over dishes.

"Who can blame her?" Louise said and immediately realized the impropriety of gossiping with staff about her host's domestic setup. "Well, I won't keep you, Amita. Thanks so much for helping out." And promptly felt condescending.

"That's okay. I need the money. Once in a while, it's fine. I couldn't stick it full-time like Lilly." The glance she shot at the woman clattering dishes at the other end mixed youthful superiority with compassion.

"We all have our reasons for keeping a job," Louise said, unsure how to prompt this girl to get on with her temporary job.

"Lilly sure does," Amita remarked, eyes narrowing in a frown that didn't mar her pretty face. Then she broke into a sweet laugh. "Listen to me, standing here chatting. Good thing the boss is inside ranting at his nephew. He's so cute."

"Who? Your boss?"

Amita's pearly laugh made Lilly scowl at them from afar.

"Oops. I'd better get going." Amita clattered cutlery onto plates, piling them haphazardly on a tray. Hoisting the load, she grinned at Louise. "Not him. The nephew, of course."

Louise smiled. "Too late. Sergeant Marpel is married, baby and all."

Mouth agape, Amita almost dropped the tray. "A cop? Omigod. I'd no idea." With that, she rushed off to the side door.

'No fan of police,' thought Louise, and bent to Shadow sprawled under the table, snoring peacefully. His moist snout rested on her foot. She stroked his silky cranium with two fingertips.

"Time to wake up," she murmured. "My foot's asleep."

Just as Shadow scrabbled his nails on the patio's fieldstone tiles, Louise heard Lilly's, "Ma'am?" from above. Straightening, she knocked her head on the table's edge.

"Ouch," she groaned.

"Sorry, Ms. Penfold. I didn't mean to scare you." Lilly stood close, her face bland.

"Not to worry. No harm done." What did the woman want, anyway? Louise frowned at the table. "Amita tidied already."

"I know. It's just Mr. Arcadia doesn't like us gossiping with his guests."

"No fraternization?" Louise chose the word with care. "Surely that's an outdated restriction. As a modern young person, Amita is free to speak her mind."

"Not while she's paid to serve." Lilly's colorless voice conveyed censure. "I'm the housekeeper. Mr. Arcadia holds me responsible for the hired help."

"But not for the guests," Louise countered, getting irked. "I take full responsibility for chatting up the young woman. She's a well-mannered person and could hardly avoid responding without being discourteous."

The housekeeper's features darkened. "Easy for you to say," she muttered.

Surprised at such treatment of a houseguest, Louise stood up and grabbed Shadow's collar. His broad chest rumbled with a low growl at the change of atmosphere.

In a calmer tone, Louise said, "I'm willing to defend Amita's courteous action if Mr. Arcadia questions it. Right now, my dog and I intend to enjoy this sunny weekend. If you'll excuse us."

Lilly's face shuttered, and the square jaw set as she stepped back to let them pass.

The encounter had rattled Louise more than she cared to admit. Though she could see the housekeeper's side, Amita struck her as a bright and cheerful person to employ. Still young, probably only 16 or 17, it was perfectly natural for the girl to chat freely. Well, Louise wouldn't get her into more trouble by encouraging gossip.

Shadow rubbed his ear on her leg. Her hand reached to pat his head. "Come. We'll see what Nora wants to do this afternoon."

Even without a leash, the pooch trotted at heel. He seemed a little wary of the terrain and so many unfamiliar bipeds.

When the vicar spotted their approach, his studious features broke into an angelic smile. He rushed over, beaming; the posy held out at arm's length.

"Let me arrange a chair for you, Louise." For a moment, he frowned at the bouquet in his hand before his brow cleared. Two steps, and he offered it with a dashing bow to his wife. "My dear, a token of my affection."

Too involved in speaking earnestly to Nora, Wilma waved a dismissive palm.

The graceful and attentive Mrs. Norton, however, fluted delightedly, "What a lovely gesture. You're quite the romantic, Dr. Brown." She leaned toward Mrs. Brown as if imparting a secret. "Count your blessings, Wilma. Not every husband is so gallant."

Noting her spouse, Wilma shifted her ample weight in the king-sized Muskoka chair and tilted her head back to regard the beaming vicar. An affectionate smile flashed across the majestic features.

"Kind of you, Vicar," she said. She glanced at his hand, clutching the posy. "They'll wilt without water."

Behind the spectacles, Dr. Brown's blue eyes dulled.

"How about popping them into a water glass?" Louise suggested and pointed to the array of glasses the staff hadn't removed from a low table.

"Splendid idea." The vicar rushed forth, carrying his token of love like a holy relic.

Unsure she was interrupting a confidential conversation, Louise sank into another Muskoka chair, a little off to the side. Its wooden slats dug into the back of her knees. She motioned for Shadow to lie down at a prudent distance from Mrs. Brown and gazed at the house as if admiring its architecture. Raymond strode out onto the patio. Seeing their group on the lawn, he hurried off onto the path circling the house like a man chased by furies.

'Oh, my,' thought Louise. 'The tête à tête with Uncle Tony went awry.'

Oblivious to her presence, Mrs. Brown spoke sharply to Nora. "You are missing the point. If it weren't for that man's stinginess, Babette would pull her weight. Now he wants her to quit. We won't see another penny and lose her network connections."

Nora wriggled her slim body in the deep wooden chair. Her hands, pale and veined, smoothed the fabric of her trousers. She spared Louise an apologetic glance and opted for clemency. "Let's not overreact. I know Antonio. His anger is easily triggered. Babette can handle him." With a tiny trilling laugh, she said, "After all, she's done so for decades."

"Of course you know them well," Wilma allowed. "Their donations used to be quite generous." Her chest heaved with a sigh. "Now they've shrunk to a trifle." She drummed her fingers on the wooden armrest. "I'd expected her to increase the fundraising activities. If she pulls out now, it will jeopardize our goals."

"Just let him simmer down, Wilma," Nora said. "He's preoccupied with business at present. Least said, soonest mended."

Wilma harrumphed. "Never works where donors are concerned. Relentless marketing is key. You know that." Her fingers drummed faster. "I'll have a word with him tonight. Dinner mellows his type."

Louise, who'd listened quietly, had her doubts.

So apparently had Nora. "Oh, I don't think that's a good idea, Wilma. Antonio's in a volatile mood today. Wait until tomorrow. See how he feels."

"Nora, it's not a bout of flu or an upset stomach we're talking about. If anything, it's chronic."

Wilma waggled her head. "How the wife can stand it is beyond my comprehension. Completely under his thumb. No backbone. I'd drop him rather than our Foundation."

Her own divorce, albeit from a cheating husband, still fresh in her mind, Louise silently agreed. No woman should let herself be dominated by a man.

"Not every woman has the strength to stand up for herself," Nora said. "Financial dependence and love are strange advisers. Babs gave up her acting career for love––just like me. Dear Hank, of course, was a wonderful person."

A wistful expression saddened Mrs. Norton's fair complexion. The past tense hadn't slipped Louise's notice. Now mentally and physically incapacitated in Rosewood's nursing wing, Nora's husband, Hank, probably bore little resemblance to the man who swept the young Nora off her feet.

A derisive snort from Wilma broke into Louise's musings.

"Love?" Guffawed the Foundation chair, rolling her eyes heavenward.

"The ways of love are mysterious," remarked the vicar, who stood by with his posy arranged in a water glass.

Seizing the opportunity to steer the conversation from the particular to the general, Louise said, "Weren't those the Lord's ways, Vicar?"

His gentle features creased into a smile as he nodded. "Love is a god in ancient mythology."

Surprised at the easy inclusion of pageant deities in the pantheon, Louise said, "Surely, a goddess. Aphrodite."

"Goddess, god," snorted Wilma. "I'll eat my..." Her glance darted as if looking for a metaphorical object. The small eyes sparked when they rested on the vicar. "I'll eat my bouquet if Babette dropped her career for love. Not that brief acting stint qualifies as a career. She must have married young."

"Thou shalt not speak ill of thy hostess." The vicar no longer smiled.

His wife laughed good-naturedly. "She's not dead, Vicar. You're scrambling your quotes again." She regarded him fondly. Then turned to Louise, as if noticing her presence only now.

"Don't mind Vicar, Louise. It's his way of re-calling me to my Christian duties."

"Oh, I thoroughly enjoy Dr. Brown's font of wis-dom, mixed or undiluted," Louise assured her.

The vicar, perched on the broad armrest of an-other sturdy chair, beamed at his wife. His hand steadied the water glass, balanced on his knee. "Your Christian duties are safe with me."

Wilma's guttural laugh rang with spontaneous enjoyment. She swiveled to Mrs. Norton, saying, "He's a dear."

In a kinder mood, she reverted to their earlier topic. "I know you mean well, Nora. But it's time to remind Mr. Arcadia of his duties as a pillar of the community."

Curious, Louise asked, "Is he a pillar of this community? I thought they lived in Toronto. Eagle Roost is a weekend getaway."

"You are right," Nora said. "They have a Toronto Harbourfront condo. The city is Antonio's main sphere of action."

"What exactly does the man do for a living?" asked Wilma. "Babette's cagey about it. I meant to Google him for ages. God knows how busy I am." She waggled a finger at her spouse in humorous admonition. "Don't say it, Vicar."

Mrs. Norton stroked back the silver bracelets on her arm, making them tinkle. "They run restaurants and clubs. Hank and I used to dine there when my godson's father was still alive. We stopped after Antonio took the helm."

"Adult entertainment."

They all turned upon hearing Hector Gambit's drawl. Apparently, only the vicar who faced the house had been aware of the writer's approach and nodded at him.

"Adult entertainment," Gambit repeated, "is Arcadia's line. It's called the Arcadia Entertainment Enterprise. AEE for short."

Wilma's eyes bulged, and her mouth gaped.

Gambit stepped closer and thrust a thin stack of printouts at Louise. "Here. My scribbles. Make of them what you wish. No need for mercy." His lopsided grin softened the abrupt words.

She took the sheets and frowned. "That's it? The manuscript?"

"Two chapters, for starters. Let me know if or when you're up for more. Or feel like tossing them on the slush pile."

Though his grin held, Louise saw an anxious flicker in the gray-green eyes. Not uncommon when writers face an editor, she figured.

Yet, more might be at stake for Hector Gambit.

Chapter 7

As they walked back to the patio, Louise felt Nora's fingertips tapping her arm.

"Do you mind if I take a powernap?" the older woman said. "Colloquia with our Foundation chair always tire me."

"I can just imagine," Louise said dryly and raised the sheets in her hand. "This will keep me entertained. Shadow and I will retreat to a quiet corner. Enjoy your snooze."

She held the French doors open for Mrs. Norton. The genteel face appeared fragile and strained.

"Will you be all right?" Louise asked.

Nora's petite figure instantly straightened. "Quiet time restores me. I'll rejoin you later." With a queenly wave, she crossed the living area.

Uncertain of where she and Shadow could sit undisturbed, Louise scanned the wide-open space. It offered no privacy to peruse a client's work. Though strictly speaking, neither Gambit nor Antonio was a client. Nor were they around to watch her reactions while reading.

Her glance fell on Babette's boudoir. That cozy den would be ideal. Not an option entering it without express permission. Even knocking didn't feel right. Babette might have sought its refuge when she fled with the Pomeranian in her arms.

As her gaze scanned the open-concept kitchen, Louise noticed a door-sized aperture at the far end of the sleek cabinet wall. It must open into a large space next to the boudoir.

Curious, she stepped closer, Shadow in tow. His nails clicked on the tiled floor. They were abreast of the spacious kitchen island when Amita emerged from the aperture.

Head turned to whoever was in that room, the girl jibed, "You do it too."

A red-faced Lilly pushed past Amita and hit some concealed button or lever, because the cabinetry panel shut without a sound. Focused on each other, they didn't seem to notice Louise behind the island.

"I'm far too busy to go snooping," Lilly snapped. "If I catch you one more time in there, I'll speak to Mr. Arcadia."

"That's so silly," Amita countered. "How can I get stuff if I'm not allowed in the pantry?"

Embarrassed about unwittingly overhearing their squabble, Louise ahem-ed. Their faces swung toward her. Amita half-smiled, while Lilly went blank.

"Sorry, miss," the girl said. "Were you looking for something?"

"Um, yes. Indeed, I was, Amita." Louise waved the sheets in her hand. "Is there a quiet spot where I can work? Mrs. Norton is in our room, taking a nap."

The girls' quick wit caught the underlying message. "You don't want to sit smack in the living room or at the dining table." To Lilly, she said, "Can't she use Mrs. Arcadia's she-den?"

"That's not for us to say." Lilly's face betrayed neither interest nor emotion. "Mrs. Arcadia is in there anyway."

"Oh, not to worry," Louise hastened to assure them. "If I'm not in the way, I'll use the kitchen desk here." She'd spotted a narrow ledge that held only a portable phone and a few cookbooks. The stool pushed in below it would suffice in a pinch.

"Mr. Arcadia doesn't like dogs in the kitchen," Lilly said.

"Spitz is in here all the time," Amita shot back.

"Never mind." Louise grew tired of the exchange. "Shadow and I'll retreat to the patio or lawn."

"Can I make you a coffee?" Amita joined Louise and Shadow on the far side of the island. "How can anyone mind a sweet dog like him?" She crouched in front of Shadow. "Can I pat him?"

Louise smiled when the pooch wagged his tail, velveteen eyes raised to the girl. "He'd like that. And I'd love some coffee."

Amita gave the feathery ears a last scratch and sprang up. "I'll get the coffee."

"Wash your hands," Lilly ordered with a grim glance at the dog.

Exasperated, Louise said, "Thanks, Amita. We'll be outside."

Just then, the door to Babette's den opened, and Spitz shot out with a shrill yip that sounded like the cry of freedom. She barreled around the island and zeroed in on Louise. Dancing on her hind legs, front feet pawing the air, she begged for Louise's attention.

Babette's weary, "No, Spitz. Don't bother people" did nothing to curb the Pom's enthusiasm. Their hostess looked careworn as she came close. The red-rimmed eyelids and smudged mascara spoke for themselves. "So sorry, Louise. Let me grab her."

"Oh, I love this cutie." Louise bent to calm the Pom. "What an adorable pup you are," she whispered, two fingers stroking Spitz's nose from its black tip to the black pebble eyes. Mesmerized, the dog sat still.

Shadow leaned against Louise's flank, exerting a slight pressure.

"How do you do it?" whispered Babette.

Amita's voice broke the spell. "Can she use your den, Mrs. Arcadia?"

"Er? What do you mean, Amita?" Babette asked.

"It's all right," Louise said, not wanting to bother her hostess.

Amita, however, seemed determined to champion her cause. "Lilly says the boss won't allow her dog in the kitchen. She just wants a quiet place to work."

The housekeeper scowled and busied herself wordlessly at the coffeemaker.

"I don't want to be in the way," Louise said in growing embarrassment. "Hector gave me his chapters to read. Shadow and I can sit outside. It's a lovely day."

"Oh, please, use my room," Babette said. "Lilly and I must see to dinner. Spitz would much rather stay up here with you and Shadow."

"We'd love to keep Spitz company," said Louise. Presumably, the housekeeper hated having the dog in the working kitchen below.

"That's settled then. My room is yours, Louise. I know Spitz is safe with you." Babette's deep intake of breath and slow release put her back in control. "Lilly, bring Ms. Penfold coffee and meet Amita and me downstairs."

"See you later, Ms. Penfold." Amita grinned as though she'd scored a victory. "Sorry, I forgot your name earlier."

"That's quite all right, Amita," Louise assured her.

The girl shot a triumphant glance at Lilly, who pretended not to notice. Yet, Louise saw the square jaw tighten. No love lost between those two. Maybe jealousy, she figured, when she watched a determined Babette exit with Amita via what she now knew to conceal the pantry.

"Is there a stairway to the basement kitchen from the pantry?" she asked Lilly, who scooped coffee grinds into the machine's filter.

"The pantry has a door to the stairs. Same staircase like to your room." Lilly glanced over her shoulder at Louise. "If you'll excuse me, I'll bring your coffee in a few minutes."

Taking the hint, Louise softly whistled to the dogs and retreated to Babette's den.

Water bowl checked and the door closed, she said, "We'll go for another walk later. Be good now while I work."

Used to her ways, Shadow slurped some water and sprawled on the rug. The Pomeranian dove into the toy basket for a faux fur duck and pranced around her new friend in hopes of a game.

Certain the dogs would sort themselves, Louise turned to Gambit's writing.

For the next half hour, she was so immersed in his account of Antonio Arcadia's life and business ventures, she hardly noticed Lilly placing coffee and cookies at her side.

Already, the opening section of Hector's exposé gave pause. The man, she thought after rereading it, really was out to expose. To demolish Antonio's image as "the quintessential self-made man," as Gambit phrased it.

The two chapters carried vindictive undertones. Occasional cynicism didn't surprise her. What puzzled was an indefinable sense of cracks in the professional veneer.

Distracted by her musings, Louise let her hand search the desk surface for writing material. On a second read-through, she must take notes. Annotating the sheets with uncensored thoughts wouldn't do.

"How very odd," she muttered softly. Surely, Antonio didn't need an editor to tell him how damaging to his reputation such disclosures would be. Not only to him, but to Babette, and even Raymond. No way her host had read this and not chucked the writer straight out of his home.

Conscious now of a complete lack of scrap paper and pens among the litter of glossies on the desktop, Louise opened the dainty drawers. Their content made her smile. Souvenirs, costume jewelry, lipsticks, and more mingled with squeaky dog toys. A wise move to keep the noisy squeakies for special occasions.

Amused, Louise pulled a slim drawer on the desk's side and struck lucky. A jumbo-size yellow sticky pad peeked from under a paperback, together with a pack of Biros.

The sight of the book made Louise chuckle. *The Boss' Wife*. A romance she'd edited years ago. Idly, Louise thumbed through the first pages.

Yes, the acknowledgements mentioned her name. Before returning it to the drawer, her eyes lit on a dedication added in blue ink to the fly-leaf. 'Yours forever –– T'

Thinking, 'Trouble's brewing,' she removed the sticky pad and a couple of pens and shut the drawer on romance.

A quick glance showed the dogs snoozing peacefully side-by-side. The curled black and white shapes reminded her of yin and yang.

With a sigh, she focused on Hector's effusions.

Apparently, Antonio and his brother Franco started with a tiny pizza parlor and takeout that mushroomed into several small-scale restau-rants by the mid-80s, known as the *Arcadia Slices*. Those run by Antonio soon offered more than pizza and pasta. Select patrons gained ad-mission to backrooms. These members-only venues flourished and raked in dough well be-yond what brother Franco could bake up in all his pizza ovens.

"The kid from Little Italy," a Toronto district where Italians traditionally settled, made it big. One thing that Antonio never shared in anecdotes of his humble origins, wrote Gambit, "upon whose backs his empire was built."

Louise paused in her note-taking to scrutinize the images Gambit used in line with his writing. Copier printouts rendered the grainy Polaroids blurry. She rummaged through the drawer for the dainty gold-rimmed pocket lens she'd spotted among the souvenirs.

Though weak in magnification, it helped to confirm her suspicions. A less dated photo taken with a camera, albeit under insufficient light conditions, showed a girl in a skimpy bunny outfit, half perched on an older man's lap. Another man in a loud suit leaned against the bar, grinning at the pair. Beyond a doubt, the girl was a young Babette. The grinning male with the proprietorial expression was none other than Antonio in his late 30s, most likely. On one side of the image, Louise could make out other bunnies, gyrating on a small stage.

Was this Babette's acting career? Did Nora know? Easy to find out without exposing Babette. More troubling, did Babette know what her writer guest was up to? Mrs. Arcadia showed no wariness in Gambit's presence. Yet, Louise suspected her hostess would be loath to have people like Wilma find out.

With another deep sigh, Louise hovered the lens over the grainier images. Two bore captions, identifying them as documenting a young Antonio's visits to roadside motels in Quebec, where legislation was lenient. According to Gambit, that was where Arcadia's idea for the adult entertainment enterprise germinated.

In one Polaroid shot, an intoxicated Antonio leaned on a barstool, clutching a far too young-looking dancer, clad in a frilly halter, panties, and feather boa. His lewd expression contrasted with his companion's fearful smile. Or maybe that was just the photo's inferior quality, Louise allowed and moved the tiny lens closer.

The girl's facial features reminded Louise of someone. But the lens exaggerated the pixelation. Maybe she could persuade Gambit to show her the digital version of the Polaroids.

Louise skimmed the sheets to the final section of Chapter 2, titled "The Buyout That Never Happened." The entire chapter traced the brothers' founding of the Arcadia Entertainment Enterprise. Franco ran the AEE's restaurant branch, while Antonio specialized in increasingly high-end adult entertainment, made possible by changes in Ontario's legislation.

This last section, however, didn't ring true. Or at least conflicted with Louise's impression gained from the little Nora had shared. According to Gambit, Antonio often claimed that he "took over everything" in the wake of Franco's death. Gambit, however, believed Antonio inherited Franco's share of the AEE simply through Franco's will, which left everything to the older brother. The writer insinuated, "Whether Franco meant to revise the will and never got the chance remains an open question."

This didn't match the facts as Louise heard them from Nora. Franco's will played no role. Antonio gained sole ownership of the AEE through a shotgun-type 'buy or sell' clause in the partnership contract. A purely commercial agreement that left the surviving partner in control.

Louise detected another error. Gambit stated that Franco and Natalie's fatal accident happened in Muskoka. She recalled distinctly Nora mentioning the accident was close to Eagle Roost, a few hours' drive east of Muskoka. This pointed to sloppy research.

She judged it superfluous for Gambit to disclose the surviving son, "Raymond Marpel—now an RCMP officer." The sergeant wouldn't thank him for being linked to the AEE by name and occupation.

The chapter's cliffhanger ending was darkly suggestive. "There were no hostile takeovers. Just accidents, coincidences, and inheritance."

Yet, if the original business contract contained a compulsory buy-out clause, then Gambit's version was false and Antonio's succession to the AEE fully legitimate. If it weren't Thanksgiving weekend, she could call her lawyer friend, Estelle, and ask her to trace the original agreement and how it played out after Franco's death.

Alternatively, and much simpler, she could tell Antonio to set Gambit straight. Her host, however, would tear Gambit's head off once he learned of the content of these chapters.

The thought hardly entered her mind when the roar of the very man's wrath hit her ears. Louise jumped as if caught in a guilty act. She pivoted to the door but found herself alone with the dogs. Spitz sat bolt upright, making no sound. Shadow merely opened a lazy eye and blinked.

As the echoey voice grew in volume, Louise detected a ventilation grid below the ceiling.

Her host and, from the sounds of it, a softer-spoken male must be in the pantry. Or a room wedged between the pantry and this den. Perhaps a narrow office. The other male didn't sound like Raymond. Nor the vicar. Either Gambit or Tyler Quak, she figured.

Slightly uncomfortable with what she was about to do, she inched closer to the vent, whispering, "It's okay," to Spitz, whose fur rippled in waves of agitated trembling.

Both she and the Pom jumped when Antonio yelled, "You're fired! Get out of my house. Now!"

For a split second, her guilty conscience took the dismissal personal. Ridiculous, she told herself. Neither she nor Gambit was an employee.

The answering murmur was indistinct. But Antonio's reply resounded through the ventilation channel. "You've got until tomorrow noon. That's final."

Swiftly, Louise scooped up the empty mug from the desk. En route to the door, she signaled the dogs to wait.

Once outside the den, she strode to the island's bar sink. Ostensibly occupied rinsing the mug, she watched.

And not a second too early. Fitted seamlessly in the sleek cabinetry between the concealed pantry entry and the ordinary door to Babette's sanctum, another aperture opened.

A pale-faced Tyler emerged. She glimpsed a grimace of pure hatred clenching the young man's jaws. His hand reached back, and the cabinetry panel slid into place. For a moment, he stood still. Then, realizing her presence, a tight smile stretched his lips.

"Ah, Tyler. I was just helping myself to a glass-- er, a mug of water," she babbled to help him over the awkward encounter.

He cleared his throat and pointed to an upper cabinet, yet sounded constricted when he said, "The glasses are up there. I'll get you one."

"So kind. Lilly supplied me with coffee. They are in the downstairs kitchen. So sweet of Babette to lend me her den to do some work." She smiled at him to hide her keen interest in his reaction.

His eyes widened. So, he was aware of the vent's eavesdropping properties. His, "You heard," as he came close, confirmed it.

She nodded mutely as the central cabinetry panel opened soundlessly.

"You still here?" Antonio growled.

Unsure of whom he meant, but ready to divert his attention from Tyler, Louise mustered a puzzled tone. "Oh? I've been perusing Hector Gambit's chapters. Your wife kindly loaned me her den. Just stepped out for a glass of water."

She watched Antonio closely for a telling reaction to the disclosure.

"Didn't mean you, Louise. Meant this young blighter," Antonio said. His broad jaw jutted at Tyler, who'd fetched a glass and set it on the island.

Murmuring, "Excuse me," Tyler strode to the French doors and out onto the patio.

Louise wondered about the side door the servers had used at lunch.

"What's your take on the man's writing? Any good?" Antonio's question seemed revealing.

To make sure, she asked, "Have you read Gambit's work?"

"Me?" He guffawed. "I'm not a reader. Except financial reports." He leaned over the island to fix her with his brown eyes. She could see the green speckles in the irises' rims and stepped back to increase the distance.

"Don't need a young ass to tell me about the industry," he scoffed. "No one needs to tell me how we stamped it from the bare ground."

With outstretched arms, he pushed himself away from the counter's edge and swaggered to the smoothly integrated fridge. Wrenching its door open with unnecessary force, he rummaged among an assortment of cans.

"Want one?" He held up a Blue, sporting a Canadian flag prominently above its logo. "Got imported beers if you prefer the foreign junk."

"Thanks. I'm good with water for now." She filled the glass, her eyes never leaving his face. With slow deliberation, she said, "Well, I'd better get on with Gambit's writing. Your wife's den is such a charming place to work, don't you think?"

He pulled the tab, letting the beer froth over his stubby fingers. His eyes locked on hers as he licked off the drips.

"Reeks of dog, if you ask me," he said. "Hey, I don't mean yours. Nice mutt. Quiet like. Not like that white nuisance."

"Oh, c'mon. Spitz is a lovely dog. High-spirited. Like a dancer." She laughed at the recollection of the Pom's begging-dance performance earlier. "She really loves to dance. Doesn't she?"

Antonio gulped beer. Rivulets coursed down his furrowed chin.

"Just like his mistress," he said.

"Eh? Spitz is a female." Louise marveled at his ignorance.

"One bitch is like another, is all I've got to say." He scowled at the can. Then his eyes rose to meet hers. "Present company excepted."

He slurped more beer and mumbled into the can, "What's the use if they can't produce kids?"

Louise felt the heat of anger rise to her cheeks. "Well, if you'd excuse me. The dogs are waiting. So is Hector's exposé." Her hand clenched tightly around the glass. If it weren't for Babette and Raymond, Gambit's disclosures would be the man's just deserts, she fumed.

Determined to keep her temper, she strode to the den's door, sure her host's eyes bored into her back.

Only when she was safely inside Babette's refuge, its door firmly closed, did it dawn on her.

She'd missed her opportunity to ask the odious man about his brother's untimely death. Or was it timely?

Chapter 8

A few hours later, Louise felt none the wiser. Nor did her mood improve as the weather turned the promised sunset barbecue on the patio into a dismal indoor affair.

They'd gathered around the dinner table at the far end of the living room. Admittedly, the panorama on display through the floor-to-ceiling windows provided a spectacular show of Mother Nature's prowess. Storm clouds, rimmed orange and bloodred, loomed over the bay. Distant rolls of thunder and zigzagging lightning bolts portended nature's wrath.

"Should they be out there?" asked Raymond,

seated diagonally across from his uncle at the head of the table.

Earlier, the sergeant had offered to help Lilly with the barbecuing on the deck, but his uncle's curt, "Not your job," put a stop to that. Instead, Antonio had ordered Tyler to assist. Louise figured he wanted to get his money's worth for allowing Tyler to stay until tomorrow at noon.

Now their host said to his nephew, "Don't be a sissy, boy. That storm's far off." He regarded the subdued company around the dinner table and muttered, "Ruined my plans."

As if by tacit agreement, they'd opted for the same seating arrangement indoors by the towering windows as during lunch on the patio. Only the empty seat on Antonio's left was now taken by his nephew. Plus, Louise thought, their host seemed even more combative tonight, and their hostess timid and increasingly nervous.

Babette's insecurity Louise could well understand. Though she had little opportunity to observe them together, she'd noticed Babette avoiding Tyler's proximity during pre-dinner drinks in the showpiece living room. Several times, she'd caught the young man's covert glances at his boss's wife. If boss one could still call an employer who'd fired one mere hours ago.

"People have been killed on the playing field by lightning from a clear sky," said Raymond into the silence that had descended again. His square jaw set, increasing the family resemblance to his uncle. "You are responsible for the health and safety of your employees."

"Not much longer," Antonio muttered, eyes on his wife at the far end of the table.

"And the creatures ran to and fro like thunderbolts." Dr. Brown's pulpit voice resonated indoors.

"What's that, Vicar?" asked Mrs. Brown.

"Ezekiel 1:14." Her spouse swiveled to face the window. "I looked; a stormy wind blew from the north, a great cloud with light around it, a fire from which flashes of lightning darted--"

"That's quite enough, Vicar." Wilma Brown's heavy bosom leaned forward to eye her husband across the table.

Despite the stern expression, Louise could have

sworn the matronly woman's mouth twitched in amusement.

"Let's take it as our prayer," Nora said, smiling kindly at the reverent. "We do stand in need of divine protection, cut off out here as we are."

With a jolt, Louise realized the truth of this. Perched on the rocks and isolated on the waters, the island abode presented a perfect target for lightning bolts. No fire engines within reach.

The thought triggered shivers running up her arms. She tugged at the cuffs of the soft blouse she'd donned for dinner.

"Are you cold?" asked Hector Gambit on her right.

They'd barely spoken beyond meaningless small talk when he mixed her a martini during cocktail hour. There was a certain shyness between them. He, perhaps reluctant to ask her opinion of the manuscript excerpts. And she, trying her best to prevent such an opportunity arising.

"It's far too muggy to feel chilly," she said now. "I just realized how exposed we are here if the storm moves in."

Hector glanced over his shoulder, displaying the classic shape of his skull and profile. "It's coming our way." His gaze returned to her, "You're not the type to worry about storms. This place must have weathered a few. Unharmed, by the looks of it."

Louise chuckled. "I've a healthy respect for nature's potency. City raised, I'm used to emergency services within easy reach." She smiled, aware his attentive façade gave no access to what went on behind the prominent forehead. "Since I moved to a small town six months ago, my gentle forays into nature have taught me to exert caution."

Curious about the man behind the mildly vindictive chapters, she asked, "How about you? City raised? An outdoor enthusiast?" Gambit didn't strike her as the type.

His eyes told her he was fully aware of being pumped for personal information.

"Like you, city born and raised," he said and turned his shapely head to glance at Wilma, who regaled Babette and the vicar with anecdotes of storms weathered at home and abroad.

Nora, Louise noticed, tried hard to engage Raymond and their host in conversation. With a notable lack of success. Antonio scowled at the window, and Raymond responded, stony-faced.

Louise's gaze traveled back to Gambit. "Another Torontonian?" she asked. "Or where's home?"

When he merely shrugged, she offered, "I grew up in the eastern Beaches. Before they were gentrified. You wouldn't think it to look at me, but my parents were diehard hippies." She laughed, thinking of them. "In fact, you might say they still are."

For once, this kernel of family lore failed to amuse, making her feel disproportionately disappointed.

A bitter note swung in his response. "No such colorful backstory, I'm afraid. Single mom, unable to cope. A trite story, not worth writing. Too many of them out there."

Shocked, Louise's eyebrows shot up against her will. "Surely, a single mother deserves our respect and compassion."

Gambit's forced laugh brought home how stilted her words had sounded, coming from one who'd never lacked financial resources. Her cheating ex-spouse's financial machinations had left her bruised but not destitute. After divorcing him, her editorial job, life skills, and yes, stamina fueled a fresh start with Shadow as her only dependent.

"I'm sorry," she murmured.

"Don't be." Hector's hand brushed the air lightly like shooing away her words––or a memory. His attention swerved to the French doors that Lilly approached with a tray. He leapt from his chair and, in opening the door, let her pass through.

"About time," called Antonio. "What took you so long?"

Arms braced against the edge of the table, he rose to a half-stand, frowning at the tray. It held a huge bowl of steaming corn cobs and a platter piled high with foil wrappers. Louise assumed it to be baked potatoes.

Wordlessly, Lilly let Gambit and Raymond help her unload the tray.

"Where's the meat?" her employer boomed.

Louise saw Lilly wince and withdraw to the patio,

followed by her boss's, "Don't keep us waiting for the steaks."

The vicar's mild features grew stern as he proclaimed, "Do not be one of those forever tippling wine nor one of those who gorge themselves with meat."

Mrs. Norton grasped at this diversion and leaned forward, pointing at his wineglass. "You are not a teetotaler and vegetarian, Vicar?"

"All in moderation." Affable again, the vicar smiled from one to the other. "*Proverbs* has words of wisdom for all occasions."

"With due respect, Padre," said Antonio. "Actions speak louder than words."

"Hear. Hear," muttered Gambit, who'd resumed his seat next to Louise.

Given Hector's exposé, the sarcasm he squeezed into two words took on a special meaning for her.

Wilma Brown took her eyes from the baked potato she lathered with sour cream and focused on their host. "I'm with you on that one, Antonio. Give me actions any time." She spared her husband a benevolent glance. "As I'm sure you'll agree, Vicar."

"You surprise me, dear," the vicar said mildly.

"Of course you do," his wife said, attacking her potato. Spearing a chunk with her fork, she paused and refocused on their host, whose impatient glare fastened on the patio doors.

Raymond was already out of his seat, opening the door for Lilly, who returned with the meat.

Wilma ignored the interruption. "Take charity, for example."

'Oh, no,' thought Louise. 'Don't go there now.'

The Foundation chair continued unperturbed. "Where would we be if our donors didn't act on their pledges? The world judges philanthropists by their generous actions."

Their host swung around in his seat, flapping his hand like swatting pesky bugs. "Find another sucker, Wilma. Your precious actors won't see another cent of my money. If they can't scrape a living from acting, they can go on pogey."

His glare slid into a sneer as it shifted to Nora

and on to his wife on Wilma's far side. "Or marry someone rich enough to keep them."

Babette, Louise saw, ducked at her husband's stab like under a physical assault. Nora went still. Concerned, Louise saw her friend's delicate features pale.

Purple blotches creeping up from throat to cheeks, Wilma leaned toward Antonio, almost overpowering the petite Nora with her bulk.

"Let me tell you, Antonio." Her deep voice vibrated with indignation. "Not all actors are entitled to unemployment benefits. Many are self-employed."

"Their lookout." Antonio attacked the steak on his plate, dismissing the topic.

"It's not a choice," the tenacious Theatric Foundation chair persisted.

"Sure it is." Antonio chewed his meat, then guffawed. "They are free to take on steady jobs if they want unemployment benefits."

"Like your dancers." Gambit made it sound like a casual remark. Yet, Louise knew better.

"What about them?" Their host frowned at the interruption. Then his bushy brows relaxed, and he smirked at his silent wife. "Great actors, the lot of them. Won't survive in the real world without me. Sure to put on an act at home."

Though veiled, this was getting nastier by the minute, Louise thought.

To her left, Babette pushed away the dinner plate, untouched. She sat hunched over, eyes cast down. From the faint glow below table level, and the slight stirring of the woman's arms, Louise guessed she was covertly typing. Texting Tyler? He hadn't come in yet.

"Do you know what happens to your dancers when you're done with them?" Gambit asked. Like Louise, he seemed to have lost his appetite and rested his knife and fork on his plate.

"Not my business," Antonio said, wiping the steak blood from his plate with a chunk of bread. "Expect they move on to another gig. Not as classy as mine." He stuffed the bread in his mouth and talked around it. "Else we'd keep them."

"Lower and lower they go." Gambit's tone held

no emotion. "Ultimate terminal: the street. Or the golden shot."

Arcadia laughed, apparently amused. "You do have a way with words, Gambit. I grant you that. Can't wait to hear what Louise makes of your scribbles."

"I doubt you'll find it amusing," the writer said.

A slight clatter came from the French doors, and Tyler entered with more meat.

"Scorched it, did you?" his soon-to-be ex-boss remarked with deceptive mildness.

"Still oozing for those who enjoy drawing blood," Tyler said, unruffled. "The rest is medium-rare to well-done."

The scent and sight of the piled-up meat made Louise slightly nauseous.

"Don't just stand there, man." Antonio drummed his fork on the tabletop. "Kept my guests waiting long enough."

The meat bearer scanned the table as if uncertain where to place the goods.

Raymond, who'd done his best involving the vicar in quiet conversation, rose to relieve Tyler of his load. A glance at his godmother had her shifting dishes to make room in front of their host.

Meat piled high, the man behind it holding a steak knife and serving fork aloft, Louise thought it the perfect image of a medieval glutton.

Tyler turned his back on the man and made for the empty seat between Louise and Babette.

He pulled out the chair when Antonio's "Not so fast" made him pause.

"Don't you have packing to do?" Their host's tone was silky smooth. "I suggest you get going."

Babette's head jolted up, her eyes startling wide and blue. Louise was sure her hostess barely suppressed an outcry.

When Tyler hesitated, Antonio yelled, "You are no longer welcome at my table."

A collective gasp met such public shaming.

Babette's "No!" tipped into sobbing.

"Swine," hissed Hector next to Louise.

Tyler strode from the room, head held high.

Raymond jumped up, accosting his uncle. "How dare you insult him in front of us?"

Nora rose and placed her napkin on the table, saying, "I've lost my appetite. You'll excuse me." She came to stand behind Babette and placed her small hands on her friend's shaking shoulders, kneading them gently. Her eyes met Louise's.

The vicar, who'd watched the scene unfold with evident distress, now sought refuge in his endless store of quotes. His voice rose over Antonio's jabbing at Raymond.

"Make friends with no man who gives way to anger, make no hasty-tempered man a companion of yours," he proclaimed.

To Louise's surprise, his spouse proved as erudite, continuing the passage, "For fear you learn from his behavior and in this risk the loss of your life."

"Enough Bible-thumping," cried Antonio. "I like my religion like the next man, Padre. But like you said, all in moderation."

Then he bellowed, "Lilly!" His eyes scanned the

table as if she might hide in plain sight. "Where is the darn woman again?"

A blinding flash of lightning drew their attention to the panoramic windows. The tremendous crack of thunder followed on its heels.

Babette screamed, and Nora flung her skinny arms around the woman's shoulders. By habit, Louise murmured a quiet psst, like soothing a frightened pet.

Like a disembodied oracle, Lilly's voice rose. "You called me?"

"Sir! How many reminders do you need?" Her boss rebuked her. "Show some respect."

"As you do," muttered Gambit.

The stoic housekeeper repeated her question monotonously, with a marked pause before adding, 'sir.'

"Clear the table and serve dessert," Antonio ordered.

Torrential rain drummed against the windowpanes.

In one voice, the guests declined the offer of

dessert in the wake of an aborted dinner. The mood had soured too much for sweets.

Chapter 9

It was after eight-thirty when Louise and Nora retreated to their room. The atmosphere down-stairs had deteriorated at an alarming pace. Like the Browns, they'd made excuses to withdraw for an early night.

Shadow would need one more business trip later, thought Louise as she glanced out the rain-spattered window. Lightning streaked across the bay. With luck, the storm might abate by then. Though thunderstorm warnings were in effect for the entire night now.

Next to her, Nora bustled with the tiny electric kettle they'd discovered in the cabinet next to the mini fridge, together with an assortment of tea and instant coffee pouches.

Chocolate or protein bars would come in handy, Louise thought with regret for not having brought any. At table, their host's foul mood and incessant needling had killed her appetite. Now, her stomach growled.

A knock on the door interrupted her reflections.

"Come in, Raymond," fluted Nora's soprano.

Shadow raced ahead of Louise, who'd just opened a bag of salmon dog treats. The fishy scent rose to her nose.

When she opened the door, Raymond Marpel stood at a polite distance. Dressed in jeans and a sweater, he appeared diffident, as if he'd shed his professional authority with his workaday clothes.

"Do come in, Sgt. Marpel. It's your own room, after all," Louise joked to ease the mood.

"Not anymore." With forced cheerfulness, he said, "Off-duty, it's Raymond, please. Thanks for inviting me to tea."

Knowing her man and hound, Louise told the eagerly wagging pooch, "Go ahead. Say hi."

Raymond crouched, and his features cracked into a genuine grin as he came nose-to-nose with Shadow. He was much more at ease when they joined Nora.

"There you are, Raymond, dear," said his godmother, lightly waving the kettle at him. "Will you have tea or this atrocious make-believe coffee?"

"Either is fine with me," he said and pecked the genteel lady's cheek.

"Here. Let me grab that," Louise said, reaching for the steaming kettle. Noticing the doggy treats still in her hand, Louise passed the bag to Raymond. "Would you...?"

"Absolutely." He fished out a biscuit and told Shadow to sit.

Dog and man taken care of, Louise made tea and carried the mugs to the sitting area in front of the largest window. They hadn't drawn the curtains. Zig-zagging lightning illuminated the horizon, but hesitantly now, as if Nature were conserving her force.

"Have a biscuit with your tea." Nora placed an open cookie tin on the bench-like table. "They look deceptively plain. Made to order for me."

"Jeremy's bespoke Sables," Louise and Raymond said in one voice.

As Mrs. Norton's frequent visitors at Rosewood Manor, they knew the Cascade baker's delicious diabetic cookies well. Nora offered the treat with tea every time.

"Too bad you didn't bring any of Jeremy's pastries," Raymond said. "I'm famished."

"Oh, dear. Didn't you like the dinner?" his godmother asked.

"The food was fine, as far as I tasted any. The hospitality was not. You hardly touched your plate, Godmother. Admit it."

Nora clicked her tongue. "Such a shame letting food go to waste. Your uncle was in a nasty mood tonight." She wriggled on the two-seater sofa to peer at Louise. "I'm truly sorry for your sake, Louise. If I had known..."

"Don't worry about me, Nora," Louise assured her with a smile. "I chalk it up to an educational experience. Remember, I'm collecting ideas for a cozy mystery. This island setting is ideal. Wouldn't you say so, Raymond?"

His eyes widened in mock astonishment. "You write mysteries? Not only edit them for others?"

"It's the plan." Louise smiled self-consciously. "Or the dream. I'd love to write cozy mysteries."

"Hm... The atmosphere at Eagle Roost feels cozy to you?" Raymond bent to scratch Shadow's ear, who lay sprawled at his buddy's feet. "Better for a psycho thriller, I'd say."

Mrs. Norton patted her godson's knee. "The chat with your uncle didn't go well, did it?" When Raymond straightened, she peered at him earnestly. "What did he want from you, anyway? Was it about this book business Louise spoke of earlier today?"

Raymond heaved a deep sigh. "No. The old story. Uncle Tony wants me to join Arcadia. As if I ever would." Contempt colored the last words.

Perhaps sensing Louise's discomfort at being a silent witness to family affairs, Mrs. Norton explained, "Franco always wanted Raymond to walk in his shoes. To give him credit, Antonio offered to take Raymond in straight from high school.

But the boy made up his mind as a little tyke-- policeman or nothing. You never wavered, did you?"

Raymond laughed, yet uneasily. "Bloody-minded, that's me. Or so Uncle Tony says."

"Bah, your uncle never understood what draws you to policing," his godmother said. "'Gets it from his goody-good mother's side,' he used to say. He never understood dear Natalie either." Nora smiled wistfully, then turned back to Louise. "Raymond's mom was a truly good person."

At the mention of his late mother, the sergeant fidgeted. He grabbed the empty tea mug and almost buried his nose in it.

To distract from his discomfort, Louise said, "Still, your uncle must be proud to see you rise in the force. You made sergeant at a young age, didn't you?"

Raymond breathed out in a sharp burst, like a snort. Or it was the mug-effect. He rested it on the table, saying, "I doubt it. Though he thinks it's useful to Arcadia. If he could onboard me."

Even with her scanty knowledge garnered from Gambit's writing about the AEE, Louise could well imagine Antonio angling for police insider tips. Was he so out of touch with his nephew to believe him corruptible? Or was her own impression of Sgt. Marpel mistaken?

"You know, Raymond," Mrs. Norton said, hesitatingly. "You ought to learn the ropes. Babette and Antonio have no children. One day, you'll inherit his enterprise. How will you run it without experience?"

The sergeant had listened with barely concealed impatience, his expression growing implacable.

"Godmother, I dearly love you. But I disagree from the bottom of my heart. If my uncle were to bequeath me the AEE, I'd donate it to the first women's shelter I'd pass."

Mrs. Norton wrung her hands. "Dear heavens, Raymond. Don't say such things. Your father would turn in his grave. How he must have hated seeing Antonio take over everything and leave you penniless."

"I doubt Dad saw anything after he and Mom died," Raymond said dryly, yet with an edge to his voice. "Mom never wanted me to have anything to do with Arcadia. She wanted Dad to sever his ties with the AEE."

Raymond's fingers reached for the empty mug, only to replace it on the coffee table. His gaze sought Nora's. "You mean well, Godmother. You and Uncle Hank always have my best interests at heart."

"Of course we do," murmured the genteel lady and dabbed her eyes with a lacy handkerchief.

"Not sure Mom ever told you," he said, almost too softly for Louise to hear. "She'd convinced Dad to see a lawyer about how to dissolve the partnership contract. Dad wouldn't have stood a chance."

"The shotgun clause," Louise murmured, and immediately cursed herself for her indiscretion.

"Pardon?" asked Nora.

"So, Gambit mentions their contract, does he?" Raymond regarded Louise, his brows furrowed. "What else does he reveal?"

Color rose to Louise's cheeks. "I'm sorry. Forget what I said. Client confidentiality." Not formally hired, the obligation was none too clear. Still, she figured, there was a tacit agreement of nondisclosure. The shotgun clause she had already inferred from the little Nora told her about the aftermath of the accident.

"Forget I asked," said Raymond. "You're right. Dad's side of Arcadia suffered most in the 2008 downturn. People don't splurge on fine dining when money is tight."

"Didn't that hold for your uncle's entertainment enterprises?" Louise asked.

"Guys still want their girly night out." The sergeant looked apologetic. "Not my idea of fun, but it's a fact."

"Franco lost on property investments," Nora put in. "That's what he told Hank and me. You were too young, Raymond, to notice how tight money grew at home."

"I noticed all right when we moved to the apartment above Dad's restaurant." The corners of the young man's lips twitched. It didn't seem a happy memory to Louise. His gaze connected with hers. "Dad lost all but two restaurants. The apartment was above the original pizza parlor. He'd hung on to that for dear life."

"Easy to understand if it was your dad's first business venture," Louise said, though she recalled Gambit writing the brothers started it together.

Raymond confirmed it, saying, "Dad and Uncle Tony opened it in the early 80s. Dad ran it until the day he died."

"And it should have been yours after," Nora insisted.

"No, Godmother." Raymond's tone was patient but firm. "Their 'buy or sell' agreement allowed Uncle Tony to buy Dad's two remaining venues for peanuts. The profits, as they were, went to settle Dad's debts. Uncle Hank explained it to you back then."

Nora's fragile features puckered in distress. "Oh, dear. We never meant for you to overhear us arguing about it."

"No big deal. It helped to know." He smiled wryly. "Besides, kids have long ears. And teens even longer ones." His smile grew joyous. "Nina is practicing already. That's my little girl," he added to Louise. "She can't talk yet, but I bet she takes in everything Clare and I say."

Louise laughed. "Then you'd better watch out. Your daughter is giving you due warning. Anything you say might be held in evidence against you. Teens often do, as my parents would testify. They must have despaired of me back then."

At her words, the joy evaporated from the young man's rugged features. His fists clenched on his legs, and his voice caught as he said, "I'll always regret the things I said to my dad during that last year."

"Nonsense," his godmother cut in. "You and your dad got along just fine. Fathers and teenage sons go through these phases. No need for regrets. Franco had a bit of the Arcadia temper."

Not lifting his glance, Raymond muttered, "So do I."

"You seem to me a particularly well-tempered young man," Louise said to ease the tension.

His grin told her he was aware of it.

It widened when he said, "You sure didn't hear me and Uncle Tony cross swords today." He scratched the back of his head. "I tried my darndest to remember I'm here as a guest. Didn't want to ruin things for others. Especially for Babs. She's always been kind to me."

"Babette's a good soul," Nora said, making Louise wonder how well Mrs. Norton knew their hostess. "She wanted you to come live with them after the accident. Antonio vetoed it. And you flatly refused."

"'Over my dead body,' I remember yelling at him." With a rueful glance at Louise, he added, "See the temper? In my defense, he'd tried to bait me with inheritance promises. Proposed to adopt me. Said at the wake, of all places."

"Oh, my. Tactless and rather insensitive," murmured Louise.

"Uncle Tony is used to getting what he wants. My reaction floored him." Raymond grimaced at the recollection. "Or, more accurately, it made him explode."

"I wish you'd have told us," Mrs. Norton said. "We heard shouting from the funeral parlor's office. I remember it well. You put on a brave face, and Antonio told me to mind my own business. Typical."

She leaned forward to peer into her godson's face. "You used to like your Uncle Tony a lot when you were small. Until that horrible incident with the kitten."

"Oh, no!" Louise's reaction escaped before she realized it.

"C'mon, Godmother. Don't dig up old tales. It wasn't as bad as you always make it sound."

Raymond's words increased Louise's unease. "Now, you'd better explain, or I'll imagine the worst."

"It was horrible," Nora insisted. Reaching for Louise's hand, she said earnestly, "I never forgave Antonio for scaring the child."

"Really, Godmother. Give it a rest."

It didn't need Nora's vehement headshake for Louise to realize the former actress would never let go. She glanced apologetically at Raymond as Nora focused on her.

"You see, Louise, Natalie allowed Raymond to bring the kitten when they came up for the weekend. She didn't know Antonio can't abide cats and is ridiculously superstitious about black cats."

"Like Magic," Louise said. "But she has a white spot below her chin." No wonder the sergeant took to Magic the moment they met, she thought. "What happened to the kitten?" she asked, unsure she wanted the answer.

Both Nora and Raymond started to speak. He backed off politely.

"Antonio tried to kill the kitty." Nora flung back her arm and let it shoot forward. "Fling it over the parapet of the cupola. Right down into the lake."

Louise gasped in horror.

"Com––mon." Raymond drew out the word in exasperation. "He did not. He was just teasing me."

Mrs. Norton's tiny headshake said more than any verbal protest.

"What saved the poor kitty?" Louise asked, loathing their host more by the minute.

"I guess I did." Raymond looked diffident. "I threw myself at him with all my 10-year prowess. Bit his hand and somehow wrestled the cat from his grip. Poor Flavio might've been crushed in the process. His nine lives brought him through unscathed."

Louise's breath escaped as if she'd been the object of the tussle. "Goodness, what a relief."

"Flavio and I remained inseparable until he passed away at almost 17. My dowry when Clare married me."

"Aww, that's so sweet. Flavio lived to a ripe old age, even by feline standards." Louise liked the private Raymond a lot. Far more than the bossy Sgt. Marpel.

Raymond's hand reached to scratch Shadow's ears, whispering, "Gotta go, buddy." He gazed at Nora. "You look bushed, Godmama. Early bed for you."

"Oh, you silly boy." Mrs. Norton reached as if to slap his hand. "Don't tell an old woman what to do." Still, she took the offered hand to help her get up and smiled when he kissed her cheeks.

As Louise and the pooch accompanied him to the door, Raymond said, "Would you like me to take Shadow for a quick outing? Save you the bother later."

"My, that's kind of you. I appreciate it." She handed him the leash and closed the door softly after man and dog.

Behind her, Louise heard Mrs. Norton draw the curtains.

Inside Louise's mind, a conviction formed. Raymond's godmother saw the car accident that killed his parents as a cold case and revisited Eagle Roost to reopen the case--bringing in Louise to righten past injustice.

Louise blew out pent-up air. Her dramatizing friend suspected their host of fratricide.

Chapter 10

Hours later, anxious whining reached Louise's slumbering mind. Semi-conscious, her lips *psst* to shush. A cold, moist touch brushing her cheek made her blink. With a start, she sat up.

"What's wrong?" she whispered, warding off the dark furry head that nudged her.

In the darkness, she heard a snorting snore. Memory flooded back. The unaccustomed room. Eagle Roost. Her roommate for the night.

Louise's hand searched for the phone on the nightstand. The screen lit up. 12:43 a.m.

Shadow whined softly, rocking back and forth in tiny, impatient steps.

There was nothing for it. Unusual as it was for the pooch to demand a nighttime bathroom trip, she couldn't let him disturb Nora. Deviation from his routine and the day's doggy excitements might cause an upset stomach.

Resigned, Louise grabbed her phone, slipped into her trousers and shoes, and pulled a jacket over her PJs. Leash firmly hooked to Shadow's collar, she eased open the door.

As she trod softly across to the staircase entry, she caught movement at the opposite end of the hallway. Someone else was still up. She couldn't tell who but felt glad not to have turned on the light. Sleep-ruffled, PJ showing under her jacket and pants, she wasn't in the mood for midnight chitchat. Whoever it was walked the other way.

The stairwell door closed with a gentle click behind her and the dog. Rather than switching on the light and drawing attention to their late-night outing, she used her phone's flash to illuminate the steps.

Shadow's nails clicked unnaturally loud when they reached the tiled lower landing. He whimpered again when she stopped to pull up her hood in case it rained.

"Poor boy. Hang on another moment," she murmured. As she unbolted the door, she told the pooch, "Be quick, and let's hope no one locks us out."

A steady drizzle met them in the darkness. Shadow stood still, nose raised to sniff the air. The weak lamp above the side door glowed amber in the mist. Moisture magnified the scent of decaying leaves.

"Don't just stand there," Louise muttered and took a few steps to prompt him to get on with business.

Nose to the ground now, the pooch took the lead and pulled her toward the front of the building. When he made a beeline for the opposite wing, Louise put on the brakes. "Whoa--we're not going for a hike."

Maybe Raymond took Shadow down the path to the boathouse earlier. She refused to do so now. A sharp order to heel brought the dog back in line, albeit under whining protest.

"What's wrong with you tonight? You won't chase deer or something." No chance of deer on this tiny island, she thought. Smaller mammals, though, might forage on a damp fall night.

Distant rumble of thunder cut into her mental chatter. "We've got to go in," she said, and tilted her head back to scan the sky.

For an instant, a light flashed up on the cupola, as if shining through from its bay side.

Did she imagine it? No one would be out on the widow's walk so late in this weather. Yet, it hadn't resembled lightning as much as a flash-light's beam.

A crack of thunder made her swing around. Now she really saw lightning flash. Across the horizon of the mainland, not the open bay. Was the storm circling back?

"Stop dawdling," she ordered the pooch as much as herself. "Do your stuff and let's get back to sleep."

If sleep would come after this rude awakening.

It was past nine the next morning when Louise joined Nora in the breakfast nook.

"Did you have a nice walk?" Nora greeted her with a bright smile.

"We sure did." Louise slid into a chair and grabbed the coffeepot. "We took Spitz along to the lookout. She was on the loose and came running when we made for the stairs." The Pom's unexpected freedom had surprised Louise. "I left them in Babette's den again. Lilly said it would be okay."

"I'm sure it is," said Nora. "Did you tell Lilly what you'd like for breakfast?"

"She offered bacon and eggs, and I didn't say no." Louise grinned. "But where is everyone? Are we late?"

"I saw the Browns earlier, having coffee out on the patio. Such early birds, those two."

"What a good idea. It's a beautiful day after last night's storm. We should go out too after breakfast." Louise glanced out the window on the front side of the house and caught sight of another guest. "There comes Hector Gambit. Seems he went to the lookout," she said, glad they hadn't run into each other. She hadn't decided what to say about his exposé, either to the writer or to Antonio.

Aloud, she asked, "Did you see Antonio yet?"

"I haven't, dear. Wilma was waiting for Babette," Nora said. "It is a little unconventional to leave guests to their own devices." She leaned close to Louise to whisper, "We can only hope sleep improves his temper."

Louise rolled her eyes heavenward and nodded.

The door opened, and the aroma of sizzling bacon filled the air. Lilly placed a dish of scrambled eggs and hot buttered toast in front of Louise and added a small cast iron pan that held the bacon.

"Oh, my, that smells wonderful." Louise smiled at the housekeeper. "Thanks so much, Lilly."

The woman's cheeks moved in a semi-smile. "More coffee?" she asked.

"Thanks, there's still enough in the pot."

Lilly withdrew quietly.

"Such a glum person," Nora whispered.

"So would I be if I worked as their housekeeper." Louise kept her voice down. "He treats her like dirt."

"It's beyond me why she puts up with it. Housekeepers can take their pick these days."

"Hm, yes. Perhaps she's fond of Babette and doesn't want to leave her in the lurch," Louise said, not sure she believed it herself. "Tell me, where's your godson? Still asleep?"

Nora tittered. "Not he. Up with the birds from when he was a child. He's kayaking. Lilly told me. That's what he liked most up here as a teen." Her eyes took on a faraway look. "Hank and I signed Raymond up with a boating club in Toronto when he came to live with us. I believe he still competes there."

"No wonder he looks so trim and fit," Louise said. "Well, I'll be done in a moment. Shall we venture outside, then? The dogs will love the freedom of the lawn."

As they entered the kitchen, a cheery Amita called, "Good morning. Did you sleep well?"

"We had an early night, thank you, Amita," Mrs. Norton said. "It's so difficult to sleep during a thunderstorm."

Louise smiled, recalling her friend's gentle snoring. "Good to see you, Amita," she said, and meant it. "I'll fetch the dogs, Nora, and join you outside."

When she returned moments later with Shadow and Spitz securely leashed, Amita rushed to greet the dogs.

"I wish my dad would let me have another dog," the girl confided. "Ours is too old for walks."

"Maybe your father thinks coping with a lively pup is too tough for an elderly pooch," Louise said. "Mrs. Arcadia might appreciate help walking Spitz."

"Oh, I love taking Spitz for a run." Amita hugged the Pom, who licked the tip of her nose. "Only they don't come here that often anymore."

"Is Mrs. Arcadia up, do you know? I feel a little presumptuous taking charge of her pooch."

"Haven't seen her, miss. The boss isn't around either. He's usually all over the place when I get here."

"We all had a restless night with the thunderstorm. Well, don't let me keep you," she said and led the dogs to the French doors.

Out on the patio, she found Wilma Brown at the head of the table, ensconced behind an open laptop. Next to her perched Mrs. Norton, diminutive in contrast to the chairwoman's bulk.

The half-moon glasses perched on the tip of her nose, Wilma frowned at Louise--or the dogs-- over the lenses' rims, and asked, "Have you seen Babette? We were to meet at nine." Her chin dipped as she glanced at the screen. "It's now 9:47."

"Sorry, no, I haven't. Nor has Amita," Louise said. She inched back to the foot of the table to keep the dogs away from the Theatric Foundation chair. "I'll take the dogs down to the beach, Nora. Come and join us if you like."

She'd barely taken a few steps when Spitz pivoted in a giant leap. Ripping the leash from Louise's hand, the Pom charged back toward the patio. Hooked to the other end of the leash, Shadow put on the brakes, causing the Pom to somersault.

"Whoa, take it easy, you two," Louise exclaimed and made a dash for the leash. Then she saw Babette in the open French door.

Far from presenting the image of a gracious hostess, Babette appeared distraught. Unlike yesterday's stylish attire, she wore sweats and a loose tank top. Hair squished into a messy ponytail, her features were taut and bare of makeup.

"Have you seen Antonio?" Babette's voice was husky with emotion. "I can't find him."

"What do you mean, 'can't find him?'" Wilma's brow furrowed. She yanked off the sliding reading glasses.

Nora rose, hands stretched as if to embrace Babette, but only touched her arm. "Come sit for a minute. He's probably busy somewhere about the house."

"No, he's not. I looked everywhere." Babette shivered and let Nora guide her to a chair. The older woman took off her tailored jacket and draped it over her friend's bare shoulders.

Spitz yipped and strained to get close. Judging the dog to be the best comforter, Louise unclipped the leash. The Pom hurdled herself forward and pawed Babette's knees. She scooped up the pooch and hunched over to hug the white furball close.

Louise joined them at the table, saying, "Your husband might be out for a walk. It's such a beautiful morning."

Babette's head bent over the dog. Her words came muffled. "Antonio never walks."

"Does he go boating?" Louise asked. "Raymond is out kayaking. His uncle might be on the water with him." She couldn't picture Antonio in a kayak but easily could imagine him leading the way in the boat.

Babette shook her head but perked up a little.

"Much ado about nothing," said Wilma with a good-natured chuckle. "Husbands don't get lost."

"We'll have a treasure hunt for him if he doesn't turn up soon." Nora patted Babette's hand. "Not to worry. Did you ask Tyler? And Mr. Gambit?"

"There they are," interrupted Wilma, pointing and waving at two figures approaching from the beach end of the lawn.

Rather than Tyler, it was the vicar who accompanied Hector Gambit. Wrapped up in conversation, they remained oblivious to Wilma's beckoning gestures. At her resounding "Yoo-hoo," the vicar craned his neck like a tortoise and sped up, pointing out the women to his companion. Gambit followed at a leisurely pace.

"We have misplaced our host," Wilma greeted her husband. "Did you come across Antonio on your rambles?"

"Dear me." Dr. Brown gazed at his spouse quizzically. With a puzzled expression, he referred to Gambit. "Your eyes are sharper than mine. Did you spot mine host?"

Hands in pockets, Gambit stood at ease a few steps back. "Not that I recall. Why? Is he AWOL?" He grinned. When his glance lit on Babette's tear-stained face, his eyes widened. "You're not seriously worried, are you?"

As their hostess appeared too upset to answer, Louise explained, "Babette couldn't find Antonio when she looked for him inside the house. None of us has seen him this morning. Perhaps he took the boat for a spin. His nephew went kayaking."

Gambit nodded. "The boat makes sense." He pulled a chair away from the table and straddled it. "As everyone and his nephew are accounted for, Arcadia most likely ferries Quak to the mainland."

"Quak?" Wilma echoed. "Isn't that the young man with the boat? Then this Quak would ferry Mr. Arcadia rather than the reverse."

"Tyler Quak," said Gambit, "is Arcadia's right-hand man who got sent packing last night. In every way. He ferries no more."

Louise frowned. Apparently, Gambit knew a lot about Tyler Quak. Yet, she'd overheard Antonio giving Tyler until noon today. Did either of them change their mind, and Tyler left early? Wouldn't Tyler have said goodbye to Babette? They might have done so last night.

Her glance swerved back to Babette, whose shoulders were now shaking. Spitz wriggled to escape the woman's confining arms and dashed licks at the tear-wet cheeks.

Nora stroked Babette's shoulders, murmuring, "It'll be all right, Babs. Don't you worry, dear."

Louise felt no such confidence. A sense of foreboding threw a shadow over the bright morning. "Let's check if Amita or Lilly has spoken to Tyler," she said.

As though her firm tone was a call to action, Shadow crawled out from under the table and scrambled onto his long legs. Leash dragging, he raced across the lawn toward the beach before Louise could react. With an ear-piercing yip, the Pom literally flew off Babette's lap and into hot pursuit.

Their prey was easy to make out by a bright orange and red lifejacket. The sergeant--returned from kayaking. Unlike his usual habit, Raymond didn't stop to fuss over the dogs but fell into a jog. Spitz yipped and danced around him, delighted at this game. Shadow jogged alongside.

Louise, who'd gone after the dogs, saw the sergeant's face first and stood still.

With an effort, Raymond seemed to control his features, which a moment ago had looked distorted as if in deep shock. He slowed his pace, discarded the lifejacket, and laid a steadying hand on Shadow's head.

Wordlessly, Louise walked by their side to join the others. She felt sure she knew what was coming.

Expectant silence met them. Only Babette's features contorted as if she, too, knew what lay ahead.

Raymond crouched next to Babette's chair, gently taking both her hands into his.

"There's something I need to tell you. It's Uncle Tony."

Chapter 11

At Raymond's words, Babette froze, for once completely unaware of Spitz pawing her legs.

Louise scooped up the whimpering Pom that Raymond restrained with one arm, while his other hand reached for Babette's limp fingers. He nodded his thanks to Louise when she carried Spitz to a seat at a distance. Shadow leaned against her leg, watchful and unsettled by human emotions.

Nora stood behind Babette's chair, rubbing the stricken woman's shoulders with gentle strokes. The others gathered closer. No one spoke. Maybe like her, thought Louise, they awaited anxiously what the sergeant would say.

Raymond's palms enclosed Babette's hands as he spoke. "I'm so sorry, Babs. I found Uncle Tony down by the water. You've got to be brave--"

Louise could barely hear Babette's shaky whisper. "Is he...dead?"

"I'm afraid so," Raymond said.

An agonized sob and gasping intake of breath shook Babette's slim body. Nora bent over her, one arm slung around the heaving shoulders. Raymond made room and pulled a chair close for his godmother to comfort her bereft friend.

His professional persona took the reins. He told Louise, "Stay close and tell the others to remain here. I must call the station again."

"You called 911 already?" she asked.

He pointed to a cell phone in a see-through pouch dangling from a ribbon around his neck. "Yes, right when I found him."

"Where did you find him?" asked Hector Gambit.

Louise hadn't noticed how close behind her he stood.

"Down by the water," Raymond said. "Look, I've got to make a phone call."

Gambit made to walk off toward the shore, but Raymond's "No. Stay!" interceded. "Please wait. The police launch won't be long. My colleagues want to talk to everyone."

When Gambit shrugged his shoulders and took another few steps, the sergeant said sharply, "Gambit. I mean it. Do not leave or go anywhere near him."

Hector wheeled around. "Who are you to tell me what to do?"

At least he kept his voice low. Still, Louise worried about him upsetting Babette even further. A glance at the table showed Wilma seated on Babette's other side, apparently murmuring soothingly. She noticed the vicar was just going inside the house.

Both Louise and Raymond closed in on Hector, Louise cradling Spitz in her arms. The dog's head snuggled against her chin.

"Hector, please," Louise said. "Let the police do what they must. The sergeant is doing what is right."

At her reasonable tone, Hector's confrontational stance relaxed. His hands slid into his pockets.

Solely addressing her, he drawled, "If there's foul play, the nephew is a prime suspect. He shouldn't have tampered with a crime scene."

"Tampered?" hissed Raymond. "I found my uncle. Dead. Of course, I had to make sure before calling for help."

"Weren't you kayaking, Marpel? Was Arcadia floating in the bay? That twitch of your head tells me no. So how could you *find* him?"

Dismayed at how offensive Gambit's tone grew, Louise intervened. "Let the sergeant make his phone call and do his duty. I'm sure we all want to cooperate with the police."

Sgt. Marpel pivoted on his heels and strode out onto the lawn. Out of earshot, he yanked his mobile from the pouch. Phone close to his ear, he swung around and kept watch while he spoke.

To keep Gambit from doing anything silly, Louise talked. "Where is Tyler? Do you know?"

"Quak?" Gambit shot her a glance before scowling at the sergeant again. "What do you want him for? He's fired."

"But not gone. Unless Antonio ferried him to the

mainland. Or if Tyler took the boat after fetching Amita this morning. And left us stranded here."

"Hardly that. There's his kayak." Gambit's chin jutted in Raymond's direction. "More in the boathouse, for all I know." His brown eyes narrowed to slits. "If Quak scampered, he'll move up on the suspect list."

"What makes you so sure it's culpable homicide?" Louise asked, watching him closely. "Sgt. Marpel didn't mention foul play. Antonio might have drowned. Or had some other accident. Even a heart attack." She didn't believe so for a moment.

Gambit chuckled softly, which struck Louise as insensitive.

Her face must have betrayed her distaste, for he said, "Don't expect me to mourn Arcadia."

"You didn't like him," she stated with conviction.

"Like him? I barely met the man. Don't tell me his treatment of his wife--or the downtrodden housekeeper--struck you as endearing." His gaze swerved back to Raymond, out on the lawn.

The sergeant pocketed his phone and watched them.

"No," Louise admitted. "Antonio wasn't a likable man. Or at least not as he acted this weekend." She scanned Hector's face for a reaction while she said, "Your dislike went deeper, though."

He just stared her down. When her glance didn't waver, he drawled, "I don't like bullies. Never have. Never will. Doesn't mean I put them out of their misery."

"No one said you did." At her words, his cheek twitched in a lopsided smirk.

Raymond strode across to them. Ignoring Gambit, he said, "Louise, would you get Lilly and Amita, please? They can bring out some coffee and tea but should stay with the rest of you out on the patio. Try to keep everyone there. I must meet the officers out front."

"I'll do what I can," said Louise. "You don't mind if I leave the dogs in Babette's den? Out of the way?"

"Best place for them. Thanks, Louise." Not even glancing at Gambit, the sergeant hurried to the path, circling to the front of the building.

"You'll excuse me," Louise said to Hector.

"Feel it's safe to leave me out of sight?" His tone was curious rather than sarcastic.

"I'm counting on your common sense, Hector. Frankly, it would be quite foolish to play ghoul with the police arriving." Unless one wants to leave traces to mask earlier ones, she figured.

Not waiting for a response, she called Shadow to her side. Spitz wriggled in her arms, eager for doggy company. "Not yet," she whispered. "You'll get treats in a moment."

On her way to the French doors, she signaled her intention to Nora, who gave a slight nod. The vicar, apparently, had fetched tea and sat with the women.

Inside, Louise found Amita brewing coffee. There was no sign of either Lilly or Tyler.

"Oh, miss," the girl greeted Louise. "Is Mrs. Arcadia okay? It's so awful about the boss."

"Um, I don't know about okay, Amita. She's in shock. Mrs. Norton and the Browns are with her. She's in good hands." Louise moved toward the den. "I'll settle the dogs and then help you carry things outside. The sergeant wants us to wait on the patio. The police will be here any moment."

A frown rippled across the girl's flawless fore-head. "My dad won't like it. Me being mixed up with police."

"Goodness, you're not mixed up, I'm sure. Not to worry, Amita." Empty words, her mind scoffed. There'd be plenty to worry about.

Fed up with being treated like a rag doll, Spitz strained for freedom. Louise hurried to the den, checked their water bowl, and settled the dogs with the promised treats.

Back in the kitchen, she watched Amita load a tray. Casually, she asked, "Where are Lilly and Tyler?"

"Lilly's downstairs prepping lunch. Haven't seen Tyler after he dropped me off at the dock at nine." Amita's dark eyes sought Louise's. "Miss, is Tyler still leaving? Like, now the boss is gone?"

"I couldn't say, Amita. Tyler worked for Mr. Arca-dia. So naturally..." Louise left it dangling.

A calculating expression pinched the attractive features. "I guess so," the girl said.

The girl suspects there's more to Tyler's relation-ship with the Arcadias, Louise reckoned and changed topics. "Would you fetch Lilly? Tell her we need to wait outside for the police. I'll take the tray if you hold the door for me."

"Of course, Ms. Penfold." With a sweet smile, Amita assisted.

Out on the patio, Louise offered coffee with quiet efficiency. Only the Browns nodded acceptance. Gambit remained aloof, leaning against a pergola post. His favorite stance, Louise noted.

Pacing back and forth with her mug, Louise had barely tasted the bitter brew when the sergeant appeared on the path circling the outer wing. With him were a tall man in a serviceable gray suit and two uniformed officers. She guessed, Sgt. Marpel's first call prompted sending the police's speedboat. As an RCMP officer, he had clout.

Yet, Louise sensed wariness in Raymond's demeanor. Or did Raymond feel out of place in his kayaking shorts and T-shirt next to a formally dressed colleague ten years his senior? The man topped him by several inches.

As she moved closer to meet them, she noticed the man's two-toned forehead. He must often cover his sandy-brown hair with a baseball cap.

Now, his sharp glance zeroed in on her and morphed into a squint as if taking her measure.

"Louise Penfold," Raymond introduced her. "Staff Sergeant Jenkins, OPP, Louise."

Ontario Provincial Police, rather than RCMP like Raymond, Louise thought, and mumbling a brief, "Sergeant," she nodded at Jenkins. Her gaze registered the freckles on his cheeks. The kind of skin that burned rather than tanned. A man who scorned sunscreen and carried a blistering nose as a badge of honor.

His voice had a faint Northern Ontario inflection when he spoke. "Please stay with your fellow guests, Ms. Penfold."

"I had no intention of leaving, Staff Sergeant." Offended at his unspoken assumption and tone, her words cut sharply.

"That's good then." He dismissed her with a last stare. "D'Souza, tell the guys to bring the boat around and secure the scene. Go down and wait for them. Let no one come near."

The officer in uniform, brawnier but an inch shorter than his superior, tipped a finger to his hat's shield and pivoted on his heels.

"PC Lenner," Jenkins ordered the female constable, "keep everyone in sight." To Louise, who still lingered within earshot but now made to go, he said, "Wait. Tell me, is this everyone out here now?"

As she could see Amita and Lilly emerging from the side entrance to the basement kitchen, Louise confirmed. "Yes, all except Tyler Quak."

"Who's Quak again?" Jenkins asked Raymond.

"My uncle's assistant. I mentioned him earlier."

Did Raymond also mention Tyler's dismissal? Louise wondered.

"Right." The staff sergeant nodded. "Let's get on with it." His chin jutted toward the patio doors. "That way up? Or by the front door?"

"Either way," said Sgt. Marpel. "If you want a word with my aunt first, we can go through the living room after."

Staff Sergeant Jenkins squinted at Raymond. "You think I should?"

Raymond gave a tiny shrug. "It's up to you, sir."

"Right. So it is. Not our favorite task, is it?" he said, almost too soft for Louise to hear.

She didn't wait for his decision and moved on to join the group at the table. Off to the side, Hector still propped up the post. Lilly hovered at the opposite end, near the entrance to the basement, as if ready to take flight at the slightest provocation.

Next to Nora, Amita fixed a curious gaze on the newcomers.

In a somewhat stiff gait, PC Lenner moved out onto the lawn and stood as if admiring the house. Yet, Louise wagered, nothing escaped the young constable's observation.

At Jenkins's approach, Nora perked up. So did the vicar. Wilma spoke to Babette in a gentle tone Louise hadn't believed her capable of. With her lids closed, Babette leaned back as if utterly exhausted.

The lids flew open at Jenkins's "Ma'am? Mrs. Arcadia?" He introduced himself, adding, "If you don't mind, I'll have a word with you and your guests later. Your nephew will give me a quick tour, with your permission."

Babette's gaze wandered over his face. Yet, Louise doubted the dazed woman really saw him.

The weak voice and words confirmed this. "Pardon? I don't understand. Who...?"

"He means me, Babs." Raymond rushed forward, and Nora moved her chair to allow him to crouch by his aunt's chair. "My OPP colleague needs to look around. Nothing for you to worry about." He stroked her hand. "There's a doctor coming soon. Maybe you want--"

"No!" Babette's voice rose. "I don't need a doctor." For the first time, her gaze focused on Raymond. "I'll be okay, Ray." She reached for his other hand and pressed it.

Louise could swear Jenkins took it all in, a bland expression masking his interest. With the slightest squint in his slate-gray eyes, he watched the scene unfold.

Only when Raymond rose, lips sucked in as if biting back some powerful emotion, did Jenkins speak. "Whenever you are ready, Sergeant."

The two men entered the house through the patio doors. Without staring after them, Louise knew they'd aim straight for the cupola. Her mind reproduced last night's impression of a flashing light on the bay side of the widow's walk.

What lay on the rocks far below was best left unseen.

Chapter 12

Determined to put her assumption to the test, Louise strolled out onto the lawn as if lost in thought. From the corner of her eye, she saw PC Lenner shift stance, readying to interfere should Louise plan her escape. To where? A dash for the water?

Casually, Louise circled to face the house, panning the sky and down to the windows. But the daylight mirrored on the panes, making them impenetrable.

From afar, Nora Norton's raised palm drew Louise's attention. Next to Nora, Amita jumped up to help Mrs. Norton to her feet and handed her a mug. With a stiff gait, Nora trudged across the lawn.

"Here's fresh coffee." Nora's stage voice carried through the still late morning air.

When she reached Louise, she whispered, "Come. We need to talk."

"She'll stop us." Louise saw the constable zeroing in on them.

"Leave her to me," murmured Nora.

Lenner closed in, saying from three yards off, "Excuse me. Would you mind staying on the patio?"

"I'm an old woman," said Mrs. Norton in a tired voice. "All this sitting makes me stiff and hurts my back, Constable." Her hand reached for Louise's arm, leaning on it for support.

"I'm sorry, ma'am. I'm under orders to keep everyone within sight."

"You can easily see us if we remain on the lawn, Constable. You don't expect an old woman like me to make a runner?"

The constable's mouth twitched, as did Louise's. Yet, Lenner hesitated.

"My godson, Sgt. Marpel will vouch for me. He'll be quite concerned if he finds me unable to get up after sitting too long. You've met him. He's with the RCMP."

That did the trick. The constable relented with a meek, "Please stay within sight."

Behind PC Lenner's back, the exodus from the patio toward the more comfortable lawn chairs caught Louise's eye. Only Gambit remained glued to his patio post. Louise's shifting gaze diverted the constable's attention. With an "Excuse me," the PC tucked her thumbs into her belt and moved off.

"Come, while she's distracted," whispered Nora. Her fingers pressed Louise's arm. She assumed a ponderous gait and steered Louise farther away from the house.

They veered toward the dense bush border, off to the left side. Mrs. Norton bent to peer at it closely, whispering, "Check. Did we dodge her?"

"C'mon, Nora. Stop playacting. Yes, she's back by the patio."

"Good. Now own up, Louise." Nora peered up,

her head tilted to one side like a robin. "Someone offed Antonio, eh?"

Louise ignored Mrs. Norton's slide into the noir vernacular and nodded. She'd expected her friend to infer foul play from Raymond's cautionary measures. "I assume Raymond found him below the cupola's widow's walk. It's all rocks down there. Or so it seemed when I glanced out the window of the tower on our arrival."

When her friend's coiffured head bobbed in eager assent, Louise went on, "Have you ever been up there?"

"Many times when Natalie was still alive. She loved the view from the top." As before, Mrs. Norton grew wistful at remembering Raymond's mother.

"Let's go to the far end," Louise said. "The angle ought to be right for seeing the cupola."

They strolled along the border to the property's limit, where a rocky slope dipped to the beach. Leaning over, Louise spotted a red kayak moored on shore, its tie line wound around a boulder.

She pivoted and scanned the outline of the house. Half of the cupola tower projected toward the water. Sure enough, there he was. Staff Sergeant Jenkins's tall figure leaned precariously over the railing.

It didn't require Louise's nudge to draw Nora's gaze to him.

"Where's Raymond?" the godmother wondered.

"Inside. See the shadow shift behind the glass?" Louise said, barely stopping herself from pointing. "Jenkins will want to preserve the scene from contamination."

Like pliers, Mrs. Norton's fingers gripped Louise's arm. "He'll be a prime suspect. We've got to do something, Louise. Raymond would harm no one."

Though criminals in Sgt. Marpel purview might feel in harm's way, Louise's intuition agreed. Raymond didn't strike one as a killer. Yet, her mind objected, as a mere child, Raymond had wrestled his uncle on the widow's walk. Antonio Arcadia might infuriate anyone. Push them beyond endurance. Someone snapped and pushed him over the railing in retaliation.

She sensed Nora's pleading gaze and a renewed increase of finger pressure.

"Louise, I swear he wouldn't." The anxious tone belied the words.

"Um, yes. I'm sure you're right," Louise mumbled.

The petite lady grasped at the weak assurance and persisted. "Besides, it probably was an unfortunate accident." In her eagerness, she let go of Louise's arm and pointed to the cupola where Jenkins seemed to rattle the railing with both hands.

"It's from the 80s," Nora said. "Someone might easily fall over. I bet building codes were lax back then. No mandatory height for railings."

"Um, maybe," Louise said, unconvinced. Viewed from down here, the railing reached to Jenkins's hip. "How tall, you'd say, is Raymond?"

"Why? You don't think..." Upon Louise's minimal headshake, she continued, "5'10" on his passport."

"Jenkins must be three or four inches taller. And Antonio was about two inches shorter than Raymond," Louise mused. "So the railing reached roughly to Antonio's belly. No way he went over on his own steam. Nor was he the type to jump."

A resigned sigh from Nora. "I fear you are right." The bony shoulders sagged beneath the silky blouse. Resilient by nature, she rallied a moment later. "Lots of people must hate Antonio. He wasn't a likable chap. Ruthless in business, Hank used to say."

"Nora. We're on an island. There's only us."

Mrs. Norton's eyes widened. "Oh, my God, yes." A furtive glance at the group now on the lawn. Then she said with authority, "Not Babette. Too slim and short to heave him over. Now, Wilma..." She paused, tapping her lips with a finger. "No. Wilma would be in no shape to heave anything after climbing those stairs."

"She might recover quickly once out on the widow's walk," Louise said. The Theatric Foundation chair was a bit of a bully and might have the physical strength for the deed.

"Seriously, Louise. Can you see Wilma exert herself for uncertain gain?"

"No. Not really," admitted Louise. "The vicar isn't the type either." Unless Antonio knew some terrible secret about either of them. Still, for now, she'd relegate the Browns to the back burner.

Her eyes strayed to the figure still leaning against the patio post, hands buried in the pockets of his loose-fitting pants. Not athletic perhaps, Hector Gambit was fit.

Mrs. Norton followed her gaze. "If I could see a motive, my money would be on him. What do his scribbles say about Antonio?"

Louise reached for a brilliantly crimson shrub, her fingers stroking the leaves. "Any idea what this is?" she asked.

"Don't evade, Louise. Burning Bush. And before you ask, the one next to it is called dogwood. Now, back to the Gambit fellow."

"You're putting me on the spot, Nora. I'm bound by client confidentiality."

"Bah humbug. Your client, if he ever was one, is dead. Did that writer hire you?"

"No, he didn't. That doesn't mean I can share the content of the chapters he trusted me with. My reputation as an editor--"

With a most sincere expression on the delicate face, Mrs. Norton's veined hand rose to her heart. "I'd never tattletale on you, Louise."

Dodging the expectant gaze that followed, Louise scanned the cupola tower again. Jenkins must have left. Her glance panned down to the patio and lit on Raymond and his fellow officer emerging from the living room.

"They are back," she announced.

"Who?" Nora pivoted to follow Louise's stare. "Oh, Raymond and the OPP fellow. You know, Louise, the OPP might call in the RCMP. With Raymond right on the spot, they'd detail him."

"Conflict of interest. Family involvement." Louise hated to play spoilsport.

Sgt. Marpel spotted them and beckoned.

"Lean on me," Louise murmured. "Though you've blown your cover standing with me for minutes on end. No point overdoing the frail act now."

She saw Staff Jenkins motion to Hector to join the group in the lawn chairs and stride ahead. Raymond followed, then half-turned to wave to Lilly, who stepped from the side door, in no hurry to heed the invitation.

Had the woman taken advantage of PC Lenner's inattention to slip down to the basement to prep lunch? Life went on, and people must eat even when the boss is dead, Louise reckoned.

When she and Nora reached the others, Nora's blue-veined hand rose and slid across her brow in a gesture of weariness. Louise caught Raymond frowning at his godmother's slightly theatrical demeanor.

While he hastened to pull up a chair for his godmother, Louise positioned herself behind Nora to have everyone in view.

Staff Jenkins's forefinger rubbed his peeling nose. His sharp gaze took in the guests and came to rest on the widow. Next to Babette, his chair at an angle, the vicar murmured soothingly. He comforted the stricken woman with mild words and pecking pats on her forearm. On Babette's other side, Amita listened, her expression a mixture of compassion and curiosity.

The vicar's wife leaned back in the spacious wooden armchair. Laptop idle on her lap, she fixed Jenkins with a stare that matched his own.

Maybe in solidarity with his aunt and godmother, Raymond perched on the edge of a straight-backed lawn chair instead of standing by his colleague.

Only Gambit and Lilly hovered at a few yards' distance, unobtrusively observed by PC Lenner, who developed a sudden interest in ornithology whenever Louise glanced her way.

Jenkins shifted his considerable weight from one foot to the other. "Thank you for your patience," he said. "I realize this is not how you intended to spend your Thanksgiving. I'm afraid we must keep you outside a little longer. My team needs to secure certain areas of the house."

"You mean the cupola tower?" asked Nora and received a scowl from her godson.

"What makes you say that, Mrs. Norton?" Jenkins's tone betrayed polite interest. Yet, Louise was sure he took note.

Nora clapped her hand over her mouth. With a tiny bob of her head, she pointed to Babette. "If your men won't need access to the bedroom wings, we could reach our rooms via the side entrance. We wouldn't disturb you."

"Smart thinking, Nora," Wilma said before Jenkins could reply. "Babette can rest more comfortably in her bedroom. Some of us might want our bathrooms, Sergeant."

"I appreciate that, Mrs...."

"Brown. Wilma Brown. And this is Dr. Brown." Wilma pointed to her husband, who wriggled his fingers from a bent elbow in greeting.

"Mrs. Brown," Jenkins picked up his thread un-abashed. "Give us some time. PC Lenner or another constable will escort anyone who needs a washroom break." His eyes shifted to Babette, whose doe-eyes seemed mesmerized by his squint. "First, I need a word with Mrs. Arcadia. If you don't mind, ma'am."

Wilma sat up straight. "Must you worry Babette, now? Surely that can wait."

The woman's protective concern for the be-reaved touched Louise.

"It's for Mrs. Arcadia to say." Jenkins's focus did not swerve from Babette's pale face. "The sooner we get information..." The implication dangled from a rising note.

Babette shifted in her seat and made to rise. "I'm okay, Wilma." It came almost like a squeak and didn't convince Louise or anyone.

"Are you sure, dear?" asked Nora and slid from her chair to assist the much younger woman. As did Raymond.

"It's best." Babette struggled to sound decisive.

"That's the way to go," said Jenkins. "Sergeant?" He nodded to Raymond. "Will you join us?" An order rather than a question. "PC Lenner will take down everyone's details. An officer or I will speak to you one-by-one."

Louise took a step toward him. "Er, Staff Sergeant? I wonder, would you mind if I go check on the dogs? It's been a while."

"Oh, my God," gasped Babette. "Poor darling Spitz. She must be so upset." The thought seemed to unsettle her.

"Ah, no." Louise hastened to calm her. "Don't worry. Spitz is fine with Shadow. But I want to check they have water and don't need to go out."

At their exchange, Jenkins's brows rose. Perhaps worried about losing the widow's cooperation, he said, "Fine with me, Ms. Penfold. I've got dogs at home. If they need to go, they need to go. Just keep to the lawn back here."

"Of course," said Louise.

She let Jenkins, Babette, and Raymond go ahead and leaned in to Nora. "I'll be back in a while." Then whispered, "Take note."

Nora gave a tiny nod and pressed Louise's hand.

Aware of Gambit's narrowed eyes, Louise smiled blandly as she passed him and hastened after the others.

She was just in time to see Babette push whatever opened the cabinetry panel to the concealed office space.

So, her intuition proved correct. She'd assumed Jenkins would ask for a private spot to conduct his interviews. Babette wouldn't dream of letting him use her own sanctum. The office was a no-brainer.

What Louise hadn't counted on was Babette recoiling from the opening.

Tyler emerged from within, hesitantly, as if surprised by visitors.

Chapter 13

Louise slunk sideways, out of anyone's direct line of vision. She needn't have bothered. Tyler's sudden appearance distracted the others.

"And who do we have here?" said Jenkins at his most jovial. "Nah, don't tell me. Tyler Quak, isn't it? The missing man."

"Missing?" Tyler was puzzled or gave a credible imitation. "Who are you, may I ask?"

"Police." Staff Jenkins switched to officialdom. "Where were you during the past few hours?"

"Police?" Tyler played echo.

Louise noticed he hadn't once glanced at Babette, who stood between Jenkins and Raymond. Instead, he now swerved to the latter.

"What's going on, Marpel? Isn't one cop enough for a weekend?"

"Oh, Tyler--it's Antonio," Babette cried, her voice shrill. "He is dead!"

Tyler's mouth gaped. For a moment, he remained speechless.

Louise couldn't see Jenkins's face but didn't doubt he'd be scrutinizing every facet of Tyler's reaction.

Were Tyler and Babette playing a charade? If they were lovers, Louise expected Babette would have texted him first thing when she couldn't find Antonio. If indeed she searched for her husband. Even if they weren't having an affair, calling or messaging Antonio's assistant would be natural. Though maybe not after Antonio fired Quak.

Didn't Babette contact Tyler after Raymond discovered Antonio's body? Or did the constant presence of Wilma and Nora prevent her?

Jenkins's voice interrupted further speculation. "You go straight out there and join the others,

Mr. Quak." He lowered his head, evidently thumbing his mobile, speaking all the while. "Do not talk to anyone. PC Lenner will attend to you. Ready, Mrs. Arcadia?"

He didn't wait for an answer but told Raymond, "Sergeant, show Mr. Quak the way and meet us in this... er, office right after."

A tactical mistake to let Tyler off the hook for now, Louise figured, as she sidled to the dining table at the far end of the living room, hoping to remain undetected by Raymond. It didn't quite work. Sgt. Marpel glanced in her direction as he shepherded Tyler onto the patio.

She hovered for another moment to ensure Jenkins and Babette were inside the office, then hastened along the wall to the den's door. With two steps, she was beside Spitz, who sat on the fluffy dog bed, wriggling the curved tail.

Louise crouched and stroked the dog's head, breathing, 'psst, psst.' It worked. The Pom licked her fingers and relaxed. Shadow rose and stretched. Sidling up, he leaned against her. At the risk of falling over, she hugged him with her other arm before reaching into her pocket for treats.

From the vent above floated Jenkins's voice, satisfyingly clear, telling Babette he needed to check in with his team. Then silence. He must be texting them.

A minute later, Louise's straining ears picked up rustling, followed by Jenkins's, "Good. Now you're back, Sergeant, let's get this over with so Mrs. Arcadia can get some rest. I need you both to fill me in on the... on Mr. Arcadia and his movements."

Louise left the dogs for a moment and noiselessly fetched soft chews from the desk drawer. That should keep them busy while she opted for the most strategic position in line with the vent.

"You don't mind if I record this, Mrs. Arcadia?" she heard Jenkins ask. "Aids the old memory."

The response, "Please call me Babette," startled Louise, so loud and clear did it carry over the vent. Like Nora, Babette must have received voice training during her acting career and used it at will.

At the sound of her person's voice, Spitz abandoned the chew and, ears pricked, sat still. Louise sank to her haunches and soothed the dog while listening to Babette's, "Is it Mr. Jenkins? Or how do you like me to address you?"

"Staff Jenkins or plain Staff is fine, Mrs.-- Babette, it shall be. Now, let's see." He paused as if consulting notes. "You hadn't spoken to your husband this morning. Is that correct?"

"Yes, he wasn't there when I woke."

"What time would that be? You noticed?"

No immediate answer came. Louise snuck back to her former position, just in time to hear, "Give me a moment. Sorry, I don't remember exactly. It was after nine when I came out of the bathroom." Another pause. "You know how you stare at your phone but don't see? I was thinking."

"Thinking of what?" So soft was Jenkins's voice Louise had to strain to hear.

"Antonio. He hadn't come to bed. His side was still made up."

"Was that unusual? Did it worry you?"

Another silence. Louise imagined how interesting the Staff must find an interviewee's hesitations.

"It's a little embarrassing, Mr. Jenkins. My husband sometimes prefers the daybed in our dressing room. Like when he works late or falls asleep watching TV. Or has a few drinks."

"Nothing embarrassing about that." Jenkins was noisily jovial again. "Time-honored tradition with us guys." Then in neutral tones, "When did you start to worry, Babette?"

"When he wasn't there."

"But..." Raymond interjected just the one word.

"Yes, Sergeant?"

"Nothing. Sorry, Staff, didn't mean to butt in. Go ahead, Babs."

"No, you're right, Ray." Babette's tone grew apologetic. "Raymond means I should've remembered. We put him in our dressing room for the night. The guest rooms were all taken. Nora and Ms. Penfold are in Raymond's old room."

"Ah, I see." The way Jenkins extended the word, Louise suspected he saw more than Babette intended. "How long were you in the bathroom? Roughly?"

"A few minutes. I drank some water and ... you know..."

"Right. You didn't take a bath or shower?"

"No. I intended to. So sorry, I felt dazed. You see, I'd taken sleeping pills and painkillers for a headache. I wasn't thinking straight this morning."

"Understandable. The evening, I hear, didn't go so well. Your husband..." Jenkins's voice trailed off on a high note.

"He was beastly."

The agitated tone had Louise check on Spitz, whose gnawing speed increased.

"Just beastly," Babette repeated quietly. "Even to our guests. What they must be thinking of us--" It ended in a sob.

"Nah, take it easy. It's always upsetting to recall. Sergeant, get Mrs... Get your aunt some water."

For a few moments, stifled sobs came at intervals, against the backdrop of Jenkins's soothing murmur.

The Pom grew restless. Louise kneeled by the dog bed, stroking the silky coat.

"There you go." Jenkins was all hearty again. "Have a sip. It'll do you good."

If Babette responded, it was too soft to carry across.

Shortly after, Louise heard her clear her throat, then apologize.

"No worries," Jenkins assured her. "Let me get this straight. You didn't see your husband this morning. What about last night? When did you see him last?"

"The time you mean?" Apparently, Babette attempted to control her voice.

"As near as you can tell."

"Around nine, would you say, Ray? Wasn't that when everyone went to their rooms? You were there when I left."

"Er, no. I don't think so, Babs. Nora had asked me to tea in my old room. You and Gambit were with Uncle Tony when I left."

"Ah, yes. You are right, Raymond." Babette's tone grew confident. "Lilly just came to ask if we needed her. I said, no, we're all good. Which we weren't. I had such a headache. I excused my-self a minute after."

Neither Raymond nor Jenkins responded. A chair creaked. Then a series of sharp metallic taps reached Louise.

"Right. That's the last either of you saw of Mr. Arcadia?"

"It is, Mr. Jenkins. I wish to God we could have talked after... I mean, today. Last night is not a nice memory to have of my husband."

To Louise, it sounded like Babette was tearing up. Though no renewed sobbing came.

"It wasn't your fault," Raymond interjected, only to apologize, "Sorry, Staff."

Raymond had a hard time separating the pri-vate from the professional, Louise thought. He seemed genuinely fond of his late uncle's wife. In a good way. Still, he was a police officer.

What astonished her was that the staff involved Raymond to this extent in the investigation. Did he figure he'd learn more if he kept Raymond under close observation? If so, the strategy ap-peared to work.

"Well," she heard Jenkins say, "we needn't worry you longer. Give me a moment to check with my team about--" He didn't finish.

"Is my husband...I mean, is his body..."

"Not to worry." The Staff sounded distracted. A moment later, he said, "All taken care of. Your husband's remains will go by launch to the mainland and the General Hospital. There are, um," he paused, then hastened on, "certain procedures. The coroner is in attendance now. He'll call an inquest, of course."

And an autopsy, for sure, Louise figured.

"But how--" Babette coughed.

"Yes, Mrs. Arcadia?"

Voice firm now, Babette asked, "How did my husband die? Please tell me."

"That is yet to be determined. I had no chance to talk to the doc, you know."

"Raymond?" Babette's voice rose, causing Spitz to jump up and whimper, a sound overridden by Babette's, "Where did you find Antonio?"

"Now, hold on, Mrs. Arcadia. Don't put your nephew in a conflict of interest. As a police officer, he is bound by strict regulations. You've got to respect police procedures."

"But it's his uncle we're talking about. Family comes before a job."

"Don't, Babs. Jenkins is right about this. It's his call to release information. Or not."

"Oh, Ray--"

Raymond cut in. "Hold it, Babs. Go talk to Louise. I'm sure she's figured it out for herself."

"Is that so?" said Jenkins.

Louise gulped. Did Raymond realize she was eavesdropping? No, he couldn't. Judging by the kitchen's stylish cabinetry, the den and office were part of a more recent renovation. Raymond hadn't visited Eagle Roost since the accident. Or had he?

Another thought caused her stomach to cramp. Babette knew the dogs were in the den, and Louise was looking after them. The implication of that was too obvious to miss.

Jenkins interrupted Louise's rapid cogitations. "I promise you'll be the first to know, Babette. Once I've spoken with the medics and my boss, we'll see what details we can release. So, if you'll excuse us."

A screeching sound told Louise that the tall Jenkins was pushing back in his chair and getting up.

"You take good care of yourself now, Mrs., er, Babette." Seconds later, "Sergeant? You'll stay if you don't mind."

Now what? Louise hesitated. Should she grab the opportunity and bolt while Jenkins and Raymond were still closeted? Or stay put? Departure with the dogs would be a noisy affair.

Across from her, the outer door inched open. Louise dashed to grab Spitz and motioned for Shadow to lie down again.

Babette slipped through the narrow gap. Her left forefinger to her lips, the other hand eased the door shut.

Still miming silence, she was by Louise's side in an instant. Gently, she took Spitz into her arms, burying her face in the fluffy white coat.

Part of Louise's mind worried the fine hair might make Babette sneeze, while another part fretted

about becoming conspirators in police espionage.

"Right. Let's see." Jenkins's words put a stop to further thought. Still hugging Spitz, Babette sank onto the two-seater.

"What's it to be, Sergeant?" The Staff didn't bother lowering his powerful voice. "Cop or private man? I'd like you by my side if your boss okays it. An insider, as we all know, is useful in an investigation."

"Don't kid me, Staff. We both know I'm as much of a suspect as the rest of them."

Jenkins merely chuckled.

"Except for Louise," Raymond said slowly. "She's never met my uncle until yesterday. Never heard of him until a few days ago."

"That's a sharp one," Jenkins said to Louise's discomfiture. "Doesn't miss a beat, does she?"

Embarrassed, Louise glanced at Babette, who gave her a shy smile.

"What about the others?"

"You put me in an intolerable position, Jenkins. These people are--" Raymond didn't finish.

"Do you know anyone other than your aunt, your godmother, and the editor lady?"

"No, I don't. Never met them before yesterday."

"No personal connection then except to the victim and his wife. Don't think the other two matter much."

"True." Relief swung in the RCMP sergeant's tone.

"There you go, then. That's settled. Now let's talk it over. Give me your impression. No more shilly-shallying."

"I didn't want to prejudice your inquiry, Staff."

Jenkins chuckled. "Fat chance of that."

"My impression, based on what I saw when I found him and when we were up on the cupola, my uncle didn't fall over by accident. It would take some strength to heave a man of his weight over the railing."

Louise noticed Babette's eyes widening while Raymond spoke. Hadn't Antonio's widow figured that out for herself yet?

"Depends," mused Jenkins. "Say he was leaning back, admiring the sky, checking the weather.

Easy to grab his legs and flip him over. Gravity would help."

"My uncle wasn't the stargazing type. And on a night like last? What was he doing up there during a thunderstorm? Or in the rain after?"

"Don't have to tell me. My ball game got canceled last night."

"Same here. Missed my team's game visiting up here."

"Fact is, he must have gone up for some reason. Else he wouldn't be lying down there now."

"Haven't they shifted the body? You haven't viewed it."

"Jeez, don't remind me. It's about my least favorite part of the job. Never fear. They are waiting for me, all right. We'll see this chap, Tyler...um...Quak? Right. Then we'll head down for a look-see."

Across from Louise, Babette rose soundlessly. She lowered Spitz onto the dog bed and held the now sodden chew to the dog's lips. The Pom's tongue reached for it and, after Babette's teasing withdrawal of the treat, sank sharp canine teeth into it.

From next door came the metallic tapping. Then Jenkins spoke. "You say you never met this Quak? Any idea what role he plays here?"

"Role? From what I understand, he was my uncle's assistant. Seems Uncle Tony terminated the employment yesterday. No, I'd never met him."

"So you can't say if this Tyler and your aunt have a thing going?"

At this, Babette gasped and quickly stifled it with her palm. The cornflower-blue irises stared into Louise's eyes as if seeking a firm hold.

"I know nothing of the kind." Raymond appeared to struggle for self-control. "And I very much doubt my aunt would--"

"Well, then. Let's ask the man himself, why don't we? I believe that knock is him now."

Chapter 14

Over the scraping of chair legs from next door rose Jenkins's jovial greeting. "Good of you to join us, Mr. Quak. Take a pew. Sgt. Marpel prefers the filing cabinet to rest his butt."

Louise's mental camera imagined the scene. The office space must be quite narrow, wedged as it was between den and pantry. A visitor chair facing the desk usurped by Jenkins. Maybe a shelf and filing cabinets. Was there a window to the veranda out front, like the den's? If so, that should tell Jenkins something about Tyler.

Quak's snarky response cut into her reflections.

"You left me no choice, Mr..."

"Staff Sergeant Jenkins. Gray-Bruce OPP."

The clipped consonants announced a switch to business, Louise figured, and glanced at Babette, perched on the sofa's edge.

'Goodness, what am I doing?' flashed through Louise's mind. Was her obsession with crime so out of control that it now overrode common decency? For all she knew, she was colluding with a killer or an accessory to the crime.

Her qualms were short-lived when Jenkins said, "I gave you plenty of time to reflect, Mr. Quak. Maybe you'd like to answer my earlier question. Where were you during the morning hours?"

"Maybe you'll be so good as to tell me what happened, Staff Sergeant Jenkins?" Tyler's tone straddled a fine line between over-polite and sarcastic. "Your minion made me a pariah at the lawn--gathering."

A quick glance at Babette revealed lip-biting tenseness. Did she also suspect that Tyler had barely stopped himself from saying 'lawn party?'

The silence next door emphasized the impropriety of Tyler's reaction to the Staff. It certainly preyed on Babette's nerves, Louise noted. Still as unkempt as before, with the squishy ponytail askew, there was little left of yesterday morning's poise. At some point, she must have slipped her arms into the stylish jacket that Nora had draped over Babette's shoulder. It looked incongruous, matched with baggy sweats and bare feet.

Jenkins played a long game, Louise thought, letting the silence stretch and biding his time until his quarry answered the actual question.

Another two minutes passed before they heard Tyler's voice, nervous and rapid, answering his own question. "I guess not. Fine. As they say on cop shows, my movements this morning. Got up. Brewed instant coffee in my room. Did some packing. That kind of thing you want?"

"You're doing fine. Carry on, Mr. Quak."

"Okay by me. 8:30ish, I got the boat ready. Picked up Amita––that's the temp. Her folks live down the road." Tyler sounded more conversational and confident. "The dad's a bit overprotective. Drives her to the dock and won't allow her to stay overnight for weekend shifts. You've met her?"

"I've seen Ms. Amita. Carry on, Mr. Quak."

Louise imagined the staff sergeant squinting at the interviewee. A disconcerting trick she'd noticed in her brief acquaintance with the man.

"Hm, yes. Got back here around twenty after nine. I saw to the boat while Amita hoofed it up the steps."

After a pause, his voice came fainter. "We saw you out on the water, Marpel."

Louise figured Raymond perched on the filing cabinet behind Tyler, forcing the other to swivel around to address him. The RCMP sergeant did not respond.

Tyler hastened on. "At least, I thought the red kayak was you. Did you see us? Your boss will want someone verifying my movements."

"Sgt. Marpel is with the RCMP. I'm not his boss." The cutting tone told Louise Jenkins reeled in his fish. "Ms. Amita's corroboration is good enough for me. Let's see--covers half an hour. Anyone vouch for the rest of your morning, Mr. Quak?"

"I expect Marpel told you Arcadia fired me?"

How did that fit the question? Louise wondered.

Jenkins wasn't distracted. "I'm aware your employment was terminated. Finish your story, Mr. Quak."

"Have it your way, Mr. Jenkins."

Louise rolled her eyes at Quak's petulant tone. She saw Babette's clenched hands tighten. Shadow and Spitz had gone to sleep, uninvested in Jenkins and Tyler. To them, it must seem just so much pointless human barking.

"I'm not making up a story for your edification." Tyler sounded rattled. "Arcadia gave me until noon today. So I packed. Saw to some odds and ends. Came in here--it's my desk, you know--to wrap up some business stuff. And then you came."

"What might you mean by then I came?"

"Just that. You, Marpel, and Mrs. Arcadia came to my office here. I'd expected Arcadia. But not the three of you."

"I bet you didn't." Jenkins remained neutral. After a significant pause, accompanied by the odd metallic tapping, Jenkins's tone shifted to satiny. "You saw me and my constables arrive. Couldn't miss it the way you'd be sitting. I can see the spot where Sgt. Marpel met us. Weren't you curious, Quak?"

So she'd been correct. Louise nodded, pleased with her earlier deduction and keen to hear Quak's response.

"Sorry to disappoint you, Jenkins. No, I didn't see you. Too busy sorting files or--no, wait. The blinds were down. The morning sun is right on the window."

"Interesting." The drawl made Jenkins's doubt palpable. "No blinds down when we interrupted your *sorting*."

"Nothing to it." Quak sounded sure of scoring a point. "I always close and open the blinds as the sun moves. Routine by now. What does it matter anyway?"

Upon Jenkins non-committal "Eh?" he hurried on, "Arcadia must have died before you got here, or they wouldn't have called you. The drift of your questions tells me he died this morning. It also tells me you don't think it was a heart attack."

The more Quak piled on, the louder he grew, yet received no response. Exasperated, he cried, "Sheesh, the man was ripe for a coronary. But no, you launch a murder investigation. Don't you?"

Babette's sharp intake of breath had Louise shift focus away from the vent. Wide-eyed, with both hands clasped over her mouth, the widow looked horrified. Louise fought the urge to rush over and comfort but feared the widow's frail self-control would shatter. Violent sobbing would betray them.

As if alerted by a telepathic transfer of emotions, Spitz woke and leapt onto the sofa, snuggling into Babette's lap. Shadow opened one deep-brown eye to fix Louise. She smiled reassuringly and refocused on listening.

Minutes passed without a reply from Jenkins.

The silence stretched before the Staff said, "My apologies, Mr. Quak. Message from my team. I must join them shortly. As to your question, it's standard procedure with us in cases of unexpected death to rule out homicide first."

"So you assume murder before--"

"Hold on, Mr. Quak. Homicide merely means 'death by human action.' Unintentional or intentional. Culpable or not. For the record, all murders are homicides. But only a fraction of homicides turn out to be murders. We've got to leave all options open and eliminate them one by one. That clear?"

"Yes, admirably so. Then he died this morning?"

"We've got to wait for the pathologist to tell us, won't we?"

Based on her true crime research, Louise figured a pathologist wouldn't narrow it down to the hour or even hours. Too many variables, in particular with a body exposed to the elements. Unless someone saw a person drop dead and was qualified to pronounce them beyond resuscitation, much depended on when the person was last seen alive.

Jenkins appeared to think along those lines when he asked, "When did you last see Arcadia?"

Quak prevaricated. "Let me think. Marpel, you might remember."

"Leave the sergeant out of it, Quak," interrupted the Staff.

"Fine. Everyone can corroborate the time Arcadia sent me packing. I mean that. Ordered me to help Lilly barbecue his steaks out in a thunderstorm. Then he tells me, 'Go pack up. You're no longer welcome at my table.'"

"Ouch," commented Jenkins. "That must've hurt. Your pride and self-esteem, I mean. You must've hated him for humiliating you in front of his guests. And in front of Mrs. Arcadia. You like your boss's--pardon me--ex-boss's wife, don't you? An attractive woman."

"Leave her out of it," Tyler snarled. Then calmly, "You didn't know Arcadia. I wouldn't have stuck it for years if I couldn't handle his temper. He'd have cooled it by now and clean forgotten he'd fired me. Hell, it wasn't the first time he'd done it."

"Still--you packed your bags, Mr. Quak. And spent time this morning sorting out business. Tells me you took this dismissal as final."

After a pause during which only a rhythmic metallic tapping reached Louise's ears, Jenkins cleared his throat.

"As a matter of fact, I did know Antonio Arcadia. This is not the first unexpected death in the Arcadia family. I've been here before."

A stifled cry interrupted. Not carried across from the next room. Louise rushed to Babette's side, who sat doubled over, the dog on her lap. Spitz wriggled under the weight and tried to lick Babette's face. Louise slung an arm around the trembling shoulders and eased Babette more upright before the Pom might yip in distress.

"What was that?" Jenkins asked.

"No idea. Sound carries in this place." Tyler spoke louder than the answer warranted. He knew very well where the sound came from, Louise reckoned. "Babette's dog. In the kitchen. Yips all the time. Did you meet Spitz?"

"Hm, didn't sound like a dog to me," said the Staff.

"Anyway." Tyler sounded bored. "If you're done with me."

A chair screeched.

"Hold it, Mr. Quak. Not so fast. We know your relationship with your boss ended rocky."

Louise cringed at the unfortunate choice of words.

"I don't know about that," interrupted Tyler. "I told you--"

"Yes, yes. Arcadia might have changed his mind when you were all packed, ready to leave. Point noted." He paused.

No one spoke until Jenkins shot his final barb.

"Tell me, Mr. Quak. What is your relationship to the missus? The soon-to-be-wealthy Babette Arcadia? We can assume she'll inherit, lock, stock, and barrel, can't we, Mr. Quak?"

Babette's torso strained forward, both fists clapped to her mouth.

Spitz wriggled over onto Louise's safer lap. She stroked the dog's soft coat mechanically.

"I resent your insinuations, Jenkins." Tyler must be standing in line with the vent for his words to echo shrilly. "I'm leaving."

"Don't go far, Mr. Quak."

"No chance of that, is there? I expect your men berthed the boat and won't let us near."

"Right, you are." Jenkins's affable tone contrasted with Tyler's carping. "Thank you for your time, Mr. Quak. We might speak again."

In a swift motion, Babette turned to Louise and pointed at Spitz, her blue eyes pleading. Instantly, Louise understood, and nodding her assent, she cradled the dog securely.

Barefoot, Babette made for the door, inched it open, and slipped out.

Louise heard Tyler's voice, "You?" and Babette's soft shushing. Holding on to Spitz, she crept to the door and closed it soundlessly.

What an awkward situation she'd put herself in. With Jenkins and Raymond still next door, she couldn't leave. How much longer could she keep the dogs quiet?

"We'd better get down there." Jenkins's words gave her hope. "Doc's getting impatient. He and the coroner gonna miss their tee-off time."

"Ready whenever you are, Staff," came Raymond's voice.

"A cool customer, our Mr. Quak. Bit of an eel," Jenkins mused, apparently in no rush to get to the body.

Louise crept closer to the vent again, straining to hear. Spitz nuzzled her chin.

"I don't envy Quak. Can't have been easy putting up with my uncle's temper for years. Anyone working for Uncle Tony needed a thick skin and forbearance."

"You've got that disposition, Marpel?"

"Me?" Raymond's joyless chuckle worried Louise. "I took the alternative route. Never worked for him and avoided him altogether."

"Until this weekend." Said factual––no hint of insinuation. "What made you break your rule?"

"My godmother. I told you Uncle called me a couple of times about this writer fellow. He wanted me to check out Hector Gambit."

"And did you?"

"No. I told Uncle it's a job for his lawyers. Or hire an editor to check the man's credentials in the industry. I mentioned Louise Penfold."

"So you said. Don't see where Mrs. Norton comes in."

"Coincidence. Babette invited my godmother for Thanksgiving and said to bring a companion if she liked." Raymond sounded exasperated.

"The long and short of it, Staff. Uncle Tony insisted we needed to talk in person. Godmother told me she'd invited Louise. I felt obligated to come this once."

The explanation seemed weak to Louise.

"Why suggest her as an editor? Do you know her well?"

"Ms. Penfold has a solid reputation. I met her over a case and as my godmother's friend. She works remotely. If I'd thought it required personal contact with Uncle Tony, I wouldn't have mentioned her to him."

"That bad, eh? Well, well. Let's bite the bullet and view our corpse."

Louise didn't catch Raymond's soft-spoken reply.

"What's the best way down there? By water?" Jenkins asked.

"There's a path around the west wing of the house. Or used to be. Kind of steep down the rock face. Better than getting your feet wet going in by boat."

Jenkins guffawed. "Coroner in his Sunday best golf gear. Must have loved that one." Then soberly, "Jeez. Keep forgetting. The man was your uncle, after all. Sorry, Marpel."

"Don't be. We weren't close. I just feel bad for my aunt."

"You think his death hit her hard?" Doubt swung in Jenkins's tone.

"C'mon, Staff. You can't be married for almost 30 years and remain unaffected by a spouse's death."

"Goes both ways. Grieved or relieved."

"Or both," said Raymond.

"There's that."

Again, the metallic tapping, this time at increasing speed. By now, Louise associated it with Jenkins. Then squeaking like ill-maintained casters.

"Can't postpone the necessary evil any longer," said Jenkins. "Corpse is bound to be stiff as a rock by now. You said rigor was well advanced at 10?"

"Yes. From that and the fact his clothes were still wet but the rocks dry, I figured he was out there all night."

"Could've been in the water and clambered onto the rocks," mused Jenkins.

"I doubt it. The state of his body suggests a fall from a considerable height. You haven't seen him, but the team can tell you--"

"You're wrong." Jenkins sounded distracted.

Louise's mind echoed Raymond's, "Eh? Wrong how?"

"I've seen him all right. Coroner just texted photos. The doc fully agrees with your assessment, Marpel."

A slap, as if a palm hit a hard surface. More squealing of wheels. Then silence.

Below the vent, Louise exhaled deeply. She kissed the top of Spitz's silky head, inhaling the warm, mildly perfumed doggy scent. "You've been a marvelous girl," she whispered. "Give it another few minutes, and you two get a walk."

She fished a pouch of Shadow's favorite treats from her pocket and distributed them equitably. By the end of the weekend, the dogs would gain a pound if such bribing continued, she thought wryly.

Several minutes later, she led the way into the kitchen, dogs securely leashed. If caught now, she'd brazen it out.

No one in the living space. Exiting through the patio doors would put her under PC Lenner's surveillance. The way to the front door via the cupola tower presumably was still out of bounds. That left the side door, accessed through the pantry.

Louise tugged at the leash to redirect the dogs and searched for the magic 'open sesame' on the cabinetry wall. It took her fingers a moment to locate a smooth button that mimicked the faux wood grain.

Noiselessly, the panel swung toward her.

Illuminated by bright fluorescent light inside, she saw a figure leaning against a shelf studded with cans and boxed goods.

One look at the clothing was enough. A white apron over a plain gray dress.

The housekeeper. Lilly.

Chapter 15

The sight of the woman standing awkwardly slumped against the shelf left Louise speechless.

Alerted by the sound of the dogs' nails on the tiled floor, Lilly's chin rose, the angular face haggard as she stared at Louise. The black kerchief, holding back her hair, increased the undereye shadows and weary expression.

'Goodness,' thought Louise, 'the poor woman must feel exhausted to take a breather in the pantry.'

Or had Lilly engaged in spying activities like she and Babette? Remembering Amita's, "You do it too," Louise's glance panned the shelves on the office side. Too much stuff to see a vent hiding behind. A stepladder stood conveniently in place for anyone who wanted to lend an ear to what the neighbors said.

To break the awkward silence, Louise mumbled, "Sorry to interrupt you."

With a start, Lilly straightened and randomly grabbed a couple of cans.

"Dogs are not allowed in here, miss." Though polite, the accusing tone was unmistakable. "If you need something, tell me and I'll get it for you."

"Oh, I'm just passing through. Easiest route to the side door, I figured." Louise stepped forward, forcing Lilly either to block her path or get out of the way.

Lilly chose the latter, muttering, "It's unhygienic."

"Mrs. Arcadia won't mind," Louise said, leaving unstated that there was no boss to object now.

What a cheap shot, she chastised herself. The housekeeper must be fretting about her job. No telling what Babette might do. Sell this immense place? Live in a convenient condo in Toronto without a housekeeper? Remarry?

After putting up with a volatile boss like Antonio Arcadia, Lilly might face unemployment. Though weren't skilled housekeepers in high demand? Nora thought so.

Both dogs tugged so forcefully at their leashes when she opened the outer door, all thought of Lilly's fate fled. A brisk walk should burn off some canine energy, Louise figured, and made for the front of the sprawling building.

They'd barely rounded the corner when Spitz yipped and lunged, while Shadow stopped in his tracks, feathered tail raised.

"Excuse me, ma'am." A uniformed officer stepped into their path. "Would you mind staying in the backyard? I can't let you pass."

"Goodness. You startled me, Officer." Louise shortened Spitz's leash. The Pom appeared fascinated by the man's black boots. "We won't be a moment. The dogs can't do their business out back for everyone to step in."

"Sorry, ma'am. Those are my orders." Legs apart, he stood unyielding. The dark blue bulletproof vest and belted holster lend him authority.

"Tell you what," Louise said. "I'll just walk them quickly to the edge of the woods and back. We'll stay within your sight. Won't we?" she added to Shadow, who sat by her side.

Perhaps misunderstanding what was required, the pooch raised a paw with a woof.

A grin cracked the officer's stoic demeanor. "Shake paw?" he asked and let the action follow the words.

Spitz joined in, dancing on her hind legs for attention.

The ice broken, the officer grinned at Louise. "Make it quick then."

She thanked him and strolled toward the trees at the mouth of the trail to the lookout. From here, she had a clear view of the building's two wings and the cupola at their intersection. The path to the rocky shore at the back of the cupola that Raymond had mentioned must be where a towering Jack pine marked the drive to the boathouse.

Next to the tree, Louise spied another blue uniform, apparently guarding the entry to the path and drive. She also spotted garbage and recycling bins at that end, conveniently placed for removal down the drive.

Louise pulled a tiny roll of dog waste bags from her pocket, cleaned up after the dogs, and strolled toward the bins. The second officer already straightened as is readying to interfere. Waving the baggies for both officers to see, Louise tossed them into the bin.

Her intentions of getting closer to the investigation foiled, Louise retreated with the dogs to the back lawn.

Little had changed since her earlier departure. Nora, Amita, and the vicar conversed quietly, their lawn chairs a few yards removed from Wilma. The vicar's wife dozed in a king-size Muskoka chair, legs stretched out on a matching footstool.

Louise scanned the patio and found Hector Gambit seated at the table, his back turned toward her. His right arm moved steadily as if engaged in writing by hand.

Then she spotted PC Lenner, whose attention appeared focused on a couple by the beach end of the lawn. Babette and Tyler.

Their body language indeed caught the eye. Tyler leaned in as if talking insistently. His hands repeatedly jutted toward Babette, only to be checked immediately. Babette inched backward when Tyler reached forward.

The tableau shattered at Spitz's sharp bark. Louise doubted the Pom could see Babette from below and probably only objected to Louise's remaining rooted to the spot. Yet, Spitz's person jumped at the canine call.

With a word to Tyler, who turned abruptly and made for the patio, Babette hurried across the lawn to the dogs and Louise. With admirable flexibility, she sank onto her haunches and hugged the excited white fluff ball, lavishing kisses on the Pom's head. Spitz wriggled in Babette's grasp, licking any exposed skin within reach.

"My, what a greeting." Louise smiled at the pair.

Babette peered up at her, eyes moist but with an expression of relief. "You're so good for Spitz," she said. "I can't thank you enough for taking care of her."

"Not at all. Shadow and I thoroughly enjoy her exuberant company. Such a darling dog." Louise handed over the leash. "Sorry I couldn't give her more exercise. The front is off limits."

"Let's walk back by the beach." Babette rose. "If you don't mind, I'd like a private talk."

"By all means." Louise fell in step, though a little wary in case her hostess would raise their espionage escapade.

She waved to Nora, who'd made to get up but now sank back into the deep chair. The vicar waved back with a kindly smile and reassuring nod.

Sure all eyes were following them, Louise strolled by Babette's side back and forth across the far end of the lawn that sloped to the beach below. She'd much preferred walking out of sight on the beach, but assumed the constable would come after them.

The elevated view onto bay, gleaming placidly as though no storm ever disturbed it, dazzled the eye. Louise let her gaze drift over the gently lapping water. Seagulls spooked by their intrusion screeched and took wing. A tangy scent, almost reminiscent of the ocean, scented the warming midday air.

If it weren't for death, this might be a rejuvenating retreat, thought Louise.

"A truly beautiful place," she murmured.

"I'll miss it." The sadness in Babette's voice caught at Louise's heart.

"Can't you keep it?" she asked impulsively. They stood side by side, lost in the sun-flooded vista.

"It goes with the company." Babette sounded resigned to the loss.

"Won't you in--" Louise broke off, recalling Nora's words about Raymond inheriting.

"No." The widow's tone was decisive. "My husband wanted the business to go to someone capable of running it successfully. Our marriage contract provides a settlement for me. Enough to get by on."

Wryly, Babette peered up at the much taller Louise. A sardonic tinge crept in as she went on, "You see, Antonio's lawyers back then took me for a gold digger. I was one of Antonio's girls, as he called us dancers. The best," she said with pride.

At Louise's commiserating "Oh, my" Babette insisted, "Please don't think I minded. I was young and sure I had a future in acting." Her face clouded. "Antonio wouldn't hear of it. He was a little possessive." A distant smile softened her features.

Maybe, mused Louise, the young Babette mistook possessiveness for love. "But who––" She broke off and said firmly, "None of my business."

"Who will inherit?" Her hostess finished for her. "That's what I wonder, too." Babette stared at the horizon as if it might provide an answer.

Spitz, clearly tired of so much loitering, tugged at the leash.

As they followed the canine hint and started walking, Louise suggested, "Raymond seems the obvious alternative. Unless your husband had other close relatives."

"Not to my knowledge," Babette said. "I always hoped Antonio would choose Raymond. He's such a decent person." A sad smile flashed over her features like the ghost of a happier time. "Too decent for that industry. He wouldn't survive." Babette's hand flew to her lips. "Oh, my God. What a thing to say."

"A figure of speech," Louise consoled her. "True figuratively in Raymond's case."

"Please, Louise. Don't think my husband was always horrid like last night. I realize he seemed beastly then. I said as much to the inspector--but you heard that."

Louise had the decency to blush.

"He was a tough man," Babette rushed on. "Had to be. You can't survive--Oh, God. Why do I keep on saying this? He didn't survive."

"Not to worry. Expressions are so entrenched we can't watch our every word." Still, she had to ask, "Or do you think a professional rival killed Antonio? That would be tough. Out here, I mean."

"Yes--No. I don't know what to think." Babette grew flustered. "Please, Louise. Won't you take on the case? Find out what happened to my husband. Please."

"Me? Out of the question. Staff Sergeant Jenkins is on the case. I'm not a detective."

"But you are. Nora says so. She told me you solved that terrible case at the seniors' residence in spring when the police were baffled."

Louise hastened to correct. "Oh, that was sheer luck." Though privately she thought they'd nicely beaten Sgt. Marpel to the finish line.

"I don't believe that. Nora tells me you've solved several cold cases for your true crime writer client." Babette squeezed Louise's hand lightly. "Do help me. Please. Raymond needs your help too. The police always suspect family members first."

The widow's pleading gaze was so endearing, Louise almost gave in. Caution asserted itself. Hadn't the young Babette believed in a future as an actress? Was all this a 'distraught widow' performance?

Why then ask Louise to take on the case? An intentional misdirection?

The answer came promptly, accompanied by a searching look. "You are already invested, Louise. Else, you wouldn't have used my den to eavesdrop on the interviews."

"The dogs needed looking after." It sounded thin to Louise's own ears.

"Of course, they did. And I'm so grateful you

minded Spitz. All I'm asking is for you to continue what you've started. Please say yes."

"There's little I can do that Staff Jenkins can't do better. He has all the means at his disposal." The self-deprecatory tone didn't even fool Louise herself. Secretly, she felt flattered and well able to find out things Jenkins might not think of.

Still, the possibility of Babette and Tyler being in cahoots loomed large. Lost in her musings, she muttered, "Whatever made him go up there last night?"

"Pardon me?" Babette frowned at such a non sequitur.

"The weather wasn't conducive to stargazing or admiring the full moon. The moon didn't show at all with such a thick cloud cover," Louise explained. "So why was your husband on the cupola's widow's walk?" She winced at the association.

The widow, however, appeared oblivious. Her brow cleared. "There's no mystery in that. Antonio loved it. He claimed it made him feel like an eagle. The cupola was his idea." Her tanned features had regained their color, and a smile tugged at her lips, devoid of lipstick. "Years ago, he'd go up for a smoke every night when we were here. Now, he only smoked when something stressed or worried him."

"In a thunderstorm? It was pouring rain last night, Babette," Louise insisted.

"Thunderstorms never frightened him. He used to laugh at people who'd run inside at the golf course when they heard thunder. He loved the light show." Again, a wistful smile tinged with sorrow or regret. "When it rained, he stayed at the open door and puffed smoke outside. I don't like cigarette smoke indoors."

Against her will, Louise's eyebrows twitched. Concern for Babette's likes or dislikes hadn't seemed one of Antonio's virtues.

"You really must believe me, Louise. My husband wasn't inconsiderate. At normal times. Yesterday wasn't normal."

No one could claim it had ended like a normal night for Antonio Arcadia, Louise's mind commented.

"Any idea what bothered your husband yesterday?" she asked. "You mentioned business worries several times. Did he give any details?"

For a few minutes, they walked on in silence. Babette stared at the ground, chin tucked to her chest, as if pondering the questions.

Bored with their perambulations. Shadow trotted by Louise's side, resigned to inscrutable human behavior. Perhaps it reminded him of obedience class exercises during his puppyhood.

Spitz danced and darted left and right as far as the leash permitted, sniffing grass and snapping at airborne leaves.

Babette's pensive voice recalled Louise's attention. "When we drove up on Friday afternoon, he was annoyed at Tyler and Lilly. He'd told them to leave early and get the house ready. Tyler texted they were stuck in traffic. We were at the dock when they arrived."

As she spoke, Babette twisted the wedding band on her left ring finger, jiggling Spitz's leash. No other rings adorned the widow's hands today.

"Nothing cropped up in Toronto?" Louise asked.

Babette gave her a sidelong look. "Not that I noticed." She hesitated. "No. I'm sure it started here."

"Any phone calls?" Impossible, though, for a wife to monitor incoming calls, texts, or emails, Louise figured.

Again, Babette took her time to answer. "Maybe I'm imagining it. His mood changed around dinnertime."

"You mean on Friday?" When Babette nodded, Louise asked, "Was it just you and Antonio at dinner?"

"Tyler, of course. And the writer, Mr. Gambit."

Babette stood still so suddenly that Louise was already a step ahead. She twisted around.

The blue eyes sparkled as Babette tapped the air with her forefinger. "That's it," she cried. Startled at the volume of her own voice, she shot a glance at the patio. Then whispered, "It was him." Her head and eyes mimed a sideways stab at Gambit, who seemed to glance in their direction.

"Sure it wasn't Tyler?" Louise asked as they walked on.

"No. I tell you." Babette spoke quietly, though the others were too far away to hear. "Antonio and that writer--I mean, Hector--talked in the office for half an hour before we had drinks."

"You...um, you didn't overhear..."

With a teeth-gritting smile, Babette shook her head. "I don't usually play fly on the wall."

"Touché," murmured Louise.

"Oh, no. With you it's different. Detectives do it all the time." Almost regretful, "In movies, they have such sophisticated devices."

"I suspect so they do in real life. With less risk of being found out." Puzzled, Louise went on, "Your husband realized anyone might listen in, I take it? He didn't mind your presence in the den, or Lilly's?"

"The office is Tyler's space. Antonio found it too cramped to spend much time there."

"Still, if Tyler talks business on the phone, you'd hardly leave the den every time. You'd hear what he says."

"Oh, that. If he makes a lot of calls, I grab my earbuds and listen to music or audiobooks. Business talk bores me. I left all that behind when I married."

"I see." Louise recalled Tyler deflecting from Babette's outcry during his interview with Jenkins. "Surely, Tyler knows about the vents, doesn't he?"

A smile crinkled Babette's tanned face. "Sure he does. We joke a bit when we're there. I mean, he in the office, and me in the den."

"Er...Babette. I ought to tell you I gave the dogs some treats from your desk drawer."

With an uncomprehending glance, Babette replied, "That's quite all right, Louise. It's what treats are for."

"Um, yes. I was searching for paper to take notes on Gambit's exposé and found sticky pads. Under a romance novel in the small drawer..." Louise could virtually hear the penny drop. Her companion's cornflower eyes gulped.

"Louise! You don't think--"

"The book stuck out for me because I edited it some years ago. Sorry, but I flipped through it and saw the inscription. I apologize, but you see, I know about Tyler and--"

"Me? You think we're having an affair?"

"Isn't that what your husband thought when he fired Tyler and lashed out at you during dinner last night?"

Though Louise aimed for a neutral tone, Babette winced like under a physical blow. A tear rolled, dislodged from the blue eye, and coursed over the golden-tanned cheek. Babette's hand swiped at it with undue force.

"You've got to believe me." The violent tone caused Spitz to jump up and brace both front paws against Babette's legs.

Shadow crocked a floppy ear.

Babette ignored the canines and stood facing Louise. "Odd as it might seem, I loved my husband. He was good to me." Her voice sank to a whisper. "Most of the time." Tears brimmed over as she pleaded, "Please. Help me find his killer."

Louise couldn't help feeling impressed. So would she be if witnessing a dramatic scene on stage.

If this wasn't genuine, the woman was a consummate actress.

Chapter 16

Watched by everyone on the lawn and patio, standing with Babette, spotlighted by the sun felt stagey to Louise. PC Lenner had changed position to have them in view. Gambit and Quak observed them from opposite ends of the table. Or were they admiring the bay's grandeur?

Louise refocused Babette only to falter at the anxious expression in the deep blue eyes. The question 'Do you believe me?' still hung in the autumn-scented air.

To evade scrutiny and an answer, Louise said, "I'd better go check on Nora."

"Wait." The urgency in Babette's whisper

stopped Louise. "Will you tell me what this man wrote about my husband?"

When Louise hesitated, Babette's hand reached for her elbow as if to prevent escape.

"My husband hired you. It's only fair to complete the job for me. Antonio can't defend himself now."

"Um..." Louise stalled. No point in explaining there'd been no contract with her host. An agreement to finish the editorial job for Babette would give her a legitimate reason to question Gambit. It did not obligate her to premature disclosure of her sideline murder investigation.

With a nod, she said, "Hm, yes. You have a right to know what Gambit intends to publish about your husband and--" Louise swallowed the 'and you.' If the widow was oblivious of featuring in the exposé, there was no point in drawing her attention to it. "You'll have to tell Gambit, though."

Relief flooded Babette's features. "I'll do it now." She shortened Spitz's leash but then scanned Louise's face before aiming for the patio. "Promise me you'll keep confidential whatever you find out. Tell no one but me."

"Er, yes. Unless life or limb is at stake--"

"You won't tell the police." At Babette's worried tone, Spitz bounced up against her legs.

"If there's acute danger to anyone, we have to involve them." When she saw the glimmer of fear in Babette's look, Louise hastened on, "I'm saying it as a general point." Though her mind insisted this was far from true.

By unspoken agreement, they walked to the patio in silence. On their approach, Tyler scrambled to his feet, almost upsetting his chair. Whatever he saw in Babette's face caused him to beat a hasty retreat to the lawn's perimeter. Hunched over his phone, his gait slowed to a halt. He didn't look back.

Louise's gaze swiveled to Gambit, who glanced up when they reached the table.

Of their own accord, the dogs sought the shade under the table, perhaps bored by human senseless rambles.

Gambit half rose in his chair, saying, "Won't you sit down?"

"Not now." Babette's hands fluttered uncertainly,

indicating the house. "I must see to lunch. It's getting late."

Gambit raised one dark brow. "I don't think anyone expects--"

"People must eat." Impatience swung in the commonplace. "I wanted a quick word with you. Louise agreed to finish the job my husband assigned to her. I assume you will cooperate?"

The firmness of Babette's address astonished Louise.

Gambit closed the notebook his hand had rested on and, with deliberate care, placed his pen on the black cover. "I see," he said in measured tones. "Did Louise tell you what I wrote?"

"There's been no time for details, as you will understand."

When Babette paused, Louise put in, "Before I file my report, I want to discuss some points with you, Hector."

"I'll leave you to it," said Babette, her eyes panning the group on the lawn. "Mr. er, Hector, have you seen Lilly? My housekeeper?"

"Your housekeeper effaced herself effectively. She evaded the Argus eyes of our warden and melted away." His chin jutted toward the side door. "Down into the netherworld, I presume."

Babette's frown at this stilted speech cleared. "Ah, in the cantina kitchen. Good for Lilly." She sounded pleased with Lilly's initiative.

"You'd better ask our warden's permission, Mrs. Arcadia, before you, too, descend to the bowels of your mausoleum."

Their hostess's face puckered. Quite right to take umbrage at the man's tactlessness, Louise thought.

If so, it was short-lived. "I guess you're right," Babette murmured and strode toward PC Lenner, who'd been watching from afar.

"A pliable widow," muttered Gambit, his gaze following Babette. Then, his hands braced against the table corners. He leaned back as far as his arms allowed. His lips slanted lopsided as he faced Louise. "Okay, fire away. But do sit. You're too tall to loom over me. I'd feel intimidated. And get a kink in my neck."

Louise opted for a chair diagonally across. With her back to the house, she'd have everyone in her purview, not least Hector Gambit.

"Right. What do you want to know?" he asked.

Aware someone might interrupt at any moment, Louise cut to the chase. "The obvious question first. What are your sources? Especially on Antonio's early exploits."

"Exploits is the operator here." Gambit leaned in, only to sit back again, his eyes never leaving her face. "News archives. Bits and pieces from interviews he gave. Web crawls. The usual stuff."

"Um, a little vague, wouldn't you say? Take his forays into Quebec. You wrote about Quebecois adult entertainment venues across from the Ontario border. Hardly newsworthy. Did Antonio mention those in interviews?"

"Sleazy strip joints, or more accurately, table dancing in third-rate motel lounges."

"Exactly. So, where did the photos come from?"

"Photos?" A blank expression veiled his face.

"The one of a youthful Antonio, decidedly drunk. His arm around a minor. A girl far too young for such a place." For truth's sake, Louise added, "If the grainy printout is anything to go by."

"Ah, yes. A telling image."

"How did you acquire it?" Louise persisted.

He shrugged. "Doesn't it say? I thought I added an 'anonymous source' caption." With a disarming grin, he said, "Louise, you're a pro. You know we can't reveal sources when we promise not to disclose. Professional ethics."

"Understood." Now she leaned in. "You'll let me view the digital copies of anything you intend to publish. Solely for my clients' protection. Their lawyers might request access." A long shot. There was no telling what Babette intended to do, ignorant as she still was of her own reputation being at stake.

Louise watched Gambit pat the pockets of his baggy trousers. He withdrew a phone and let his tapered fingers scroll for a minute.

"Here. Is the one you mean?" Gambit held out the mobile. "As said, I'm not prepared to release any."

Though the screen size wasn't ideal, she jumped at the offer and stretched out her hand, not moving closer. Short of being churlish, it left him no choice but to let go of the device.

The motel bar shot was a reproduction of a Polaroid picture. Grainy still in its digital format. Louise pinched the screen, zooming in and out. Antonio's inane grin remained lewd and revolting. Close up, the girl's body language seemed a mix of allure and something else. Her shoulder shrunk forward under Antonio's grasp, while she smiled up at him. Was it the distortion from the pixelation, or was the forced smile covering a grimace of fear? Squinting to focus, Louise again had a sense of déjà vu.

Don't get fanciful, she ordered herself. With a quick glance at Hector, who gazed at the distant bay, she swiped to the next photo.

Judging from the inferior quality, the image was an enlargement. A different young woman also scantily dressed. A feather-studded diadem held back dark curls from her prominent forehead, making it appear vulnerable. Her bare shoulders showed white under the grasp of a hairy, masculine hand that seemed to dig into the flesh with a possessive grip. This time, Louise could guess the young woman's identity.

"Are you done with it?" asked Hector.

"Um, no. Would you show me the one of Antonio and... I mean a much later picture. It shows a woman in a bunny outfit at a bar with an older man and Antonio?"

Gambit chuckled softly. "The one of our fair widow in her heyday? Sure." His hand reached for the phone.

When he handed it back, the screen showed exactly the photo she'd meant. No graininess here. Nor room for doubt. Babette's young face transformed by a mask of professional enjoyment. With painted eyelids slightly lowered, the tip of her tongue protruding between voluptuous, cheery-red lips, she presented a pin-up pose of seduction geared, not at Antonio, but at the much older man on her other side. Her future husband, in a flashy outfit, with a lewd grin pasted on his face, egged her on.

"You won't publish this without Mrs. Arcadia's permission." Spoken out loud, the prospect revolted her even more.

"You disapprove?" Gambit spoke mildly. "I don't see why not. It's an indelible part of the story."

"That's monstrous under the present circumstances."

"Piety for the dear departed? Or for the grieving
widow?"

"I don't like your cynical tone, Mr. Gambit. You
may have disliked Antonio Arcadia and have an
ax to grind. Surely, his widow deserves our compassion." Her words sounded pompous to
Louise's ears. Nor was it a professional way to
react.

"Aren't we getting too emotional?" Gambit
echoed her mind's misgivings. "I intend to
capture the true story of Arcadia and the AEE.
Mrs. Arcadia chose to be part of that story.
Yes, her career began as one of Arcadia's girls.
She, unlike many others, played her cards right
and made good." He wrinkled his nose as if hit
by a foul odor. "Listen to my clichés. My
apologies."

"I'm not worried about your clichés. Nor about
the reputation of the dead. My concern is with
the living. Mrs. Arcadia has built her life. Tar-
nishing her reputation within her circle seems
needless cruelty to me."

Again, he merely shrugged.

"Tell me," Louise insisted. "Would your exposé suffer by scrapping that photo?" When his mouth twisted in stubborn rejection, she answered herself. "Of course not. No one would miss it."

He crossed his arms over his chest. His lips pressed together.

Louise knew better than to press the point. Let him stew on it.

As the silence thickened between them, she stared at the phone now resting on the table. Did the device contain even more damaging pictures? Were some of Arcadia's "girls" yet younger than the one in the grainy polaroid?

Revulsion rippled in shivers along her arms. That kind of thing was not merely utterly revolting, it yielded potent ammunition. For a blockbuster exposé and for--blackmail.

Was that what Gambit had tried while closeted with Arcadia in the office on Friday night?

Louise shook her head at the thought. A bully like Antonio would explode. Chase Gambit off the property. Make him swim for shore. Set his goons on him.

In that case, did the wrong person die?

Chapter 17

"Ah, Mr. Gambit. Sorry, Ms. Penfold, to startle you."

Staff Sergeant Jenkins's jovial address ripped Louise from her equally startling cogitations. She gaped at Jenkins like he were an alien presence. Her disproportionate reaction made the Staff squint and Gambit frown.

"Not at all," she lied. "Mr. Gambit and I were chatting about his work."

"Just what's on my mind, too," said Jenkins, at his most affable. "If you'd spare me a few minutes, Mr. Gambit, I'd like a word with you."

The writer's shoulder twitched in a habitual shrug. His chair scraped back on the flagstones.

"You'll excuse us, Ms. Penfold." Jenkins's forefinger scratched the tip of his peeling nose. "We'll go inside, Mr. Gambit."

"Will you walk into my parlor?" muttered Hector.

"Said the spider to the fly." Jenkins finished for him.

At their surprised glances, the corner of Jenkins's mouth twitched.

"Mr. Jenkins!" Babette's high-pitched cry interrupted. With Raymond at her heels and PC Lenner at the rear, Babette rushed toward them.

Spitz shot out from under the table and dashed at the trio. Raymond scooped up the dog and tucked her under his arm. Quickly, Louise motioned to Shadow to stay put.

"What can I do for you, Mrs. Arcadia?" The Staff waited. The benign expression he mustered didn't reach his eyes. They remained watchful, Louise observed.

"Your constable won't allow me into my own house." Either the quick movement or outrage at being thwarted brought dark patches to Babette's cheeks. "I must see to lunch. How intolerable for my guests to be kept out here, and no food or drink."

"Babs, don't," murmured Raymond.

"It's all right, Sergeant," Jenkins said. "Your aunt is justly upset. Not to worry, Mrs. Arcadia. My team's job inside is nearly done. Your guests may use most of your place. Mind the yellow tape. The cupola remains off limits."

As he spoke, Babette's energy, fueled by anger, seemed to evaporate, almost diminishing her in size, thought Louise. Even the irritated glance their hostess spared the constable lacked force. It sufficed for PC Lenner to fade politely into the background.

Jenkins's attention had already moved on. "Ready, Mr. Gambit? Sergeant?" Not waiting for a reply, he strode to the patio doors.

Gambit followed at a leisurely pace.

Raymond hesitated. "Would you?" He proffered the Pom to Louise and hastened after his colleague and their interviewee.

Left standing, Louise contemplated using Spitz as an excuse to return to the den.

"Louise?" Babette recalled her. "Would you tell everyone we'll have a buffet lunch on the patio in half an hour? They can freshen up in their rooms if they like."

"Of course," Louise said, and offered to hand over Spitz.

Babette unhooked the dog's leash and set her free. Spitz gamboled across the lawn.

"Let the dogs run and have some fun. They've been so good all morning. Oh, and ask Amita to join me downstairs." With that, Babette hurried to the patio entrance to the basement kitchen. From the door, she called, "Thanks for your help."

Louise assumed the thanks were for tackling Gambit rather than for running errands. She un-hooked Shadow's leash and told him to go play. He charged after Spitz, who already had enticed the vicar to throw sticks.

While Louise passed on their hostess's message, her glance strayed to Tyler, absorbed in texting, to judge by the relentless thumb tapping.

"Where's my godson off to again?" asked Nora.

"He and Jenkins are interviewing Hector Gambit in Tyler's office, I assume," Louise said.

"I see," said Nora, and looked pensive. "Wilma? You don't mind if I dash? The powder room calls." She leveled a conspiratorial look at Louise and left them with a finger-wriggling wave.

Maybe still dazed from her snooze, Mrs. Brown regarded the laptop, closed now on her lap.

"If you'll excuse me," Louise said, as Wilma struggled to rise.

Seeing the dogs joyfully engaged with the vicar in a chase for sticks, he sprinting after them like a boy let out to play, she crossed the lawn to Tyler.

When the young man noticed her approach, he pocketed his phone with furtive swiftness. Guilt at passing the news of Arcadia's death to the outer world? she wondered. Or was he eager for company?

"Sorry to interrupt, Tyler. Babette wants me to let everyone know the police are allowing us back inside. She's offering a buffet lunch on the patio."

"Lunch? How can she think of lunch at a time like this?" He seemed offended by such a triviality.

"People must eat," Louise echoed her hostess.

"I couldn't eat now." Tyler made it sound like a virtue. His expression grew eager like a smitten schoolboy's. "How is she taking it?"

When Louise let her eyebrows rise in slow puzzlement, he said, "His death."

Louise frowned. "Babette is in shock, as one would expect. Why ask me? It's you who knows the Arcadias well. I'd never met them until yesterday."

His mien clouded. "She's much better off without him," he muttered.

"I hope it's not the kind of remark you make to the police, Tyler. They might misconstrue it."

"They do that already. How can Raymond sit by when this Jenkins insults his aunt?" Tyler glared at Louise as though it were her fault. "You heard him insinuate she's having an affair with me."

"Is she?"

Despite her soft tone, Tyler appeared stung. "How dare you? I thought you were on her side."

"I'm on the side of truth," Louise said.

"You want the truth?" The angry outburst dissolved, and reddening, his face puckered. "I don't want an affair. I wanted her to leave that old bully and marry me."

"She refused?" Louise murmured.

His lips trembled. For a moment, she feared he might cry. He stuffed his clenched fists into his pockets. Louise strained her ears to understand his whisper. "She laughed. Said I'd grow tired of her when she gets wrinkly. As if she ever would."

He sounded so much like a kid whose parents refused him a favorite toy, Louise felt torn between exasperation and pity.

"Well, we all get wrinkly as we age," she murmured. Was the age difference what stopped Babette? Not according to what the woman had avowed earlier.

Curious how Tyler would react to that, Louise said, "A bully Antonio might have been. On first acquaintance, his manners seemed abrasive. His wife, however, insists he wasn't always like that.

My impression is she loved him and grieves his death."

"Loved him?" he echoed. His snide laugh drew the constable's attention, Louise noticed. Tyler seemed oblivious and insisted, "Sure, that's what she told herself to make life with him bearable. He was a brute. Would screw anyone over just for the fun of it."

Louise tut-tutted, intent on further disclosures. Time might run out for this tête-à-tête. How much longer would the vicar keep the dogs busy, and PC Lenner stay away?

Her patience worked. Or the young man simply needed to vent to anyone who would listen.

Visibly struggling to keep a violent emotion in check, Tyler broke into a tirade. "He accused me of going after his wife. I told him she'd be a hundred times better off with me. The swine said she'd soon tire of being poor again, and he'd make sure I'd never get another job."

"When was that?" Louise asked when he took a deep breath.

"Yesterday afternoon. In my office." Almost proudly, he added, "He fired me."

"Didn't you admit Babette—um—rejected you? No wonder he treated her so badly at dinner last night." How unfair not to have vindicated Babette if the two never had an affair?

"I did so," he insisted, like a petulant teen.

"Did he believe you? He certainly was in a foul mood after." For all she knew, Antonio's wrath stemmed from a dispute with Gambit, or anyone else for that matter.

"I told the bully I'd win her over." The boast was now unmistakable. "That's when he fired me. The swine couldn't stand to lose. Ever."

"Well, some people are like that," Louise said mildly.

All boyish again, Tyler gave her a shy but mildly sly look. "You think she'll have me when all this is over?"

With an effort, Louise prevented an eye roll and opted for sternness. "Tyler. This is not the time to plan a wedding. I suggest you practice reticence. Keep your distance. The police might draw their own conclusions if you––if you pursue your goal now." She'd almost said, 'act like a love-sick teenager.' He struck her as surprisingly immature where Babette was concerned. Quite unlike the efficient assistant he'd seemed on first acquaintance.

"Yeah, I will. It's what Babette said. Told me to stay away." Then he perked up. "Until all this is over."

"Um, yes. We can only hope the police will solve this case soon. It mightn't be easy."

Their talk seemed to act as a catalyst. His confidence returned. With a toss of his head, he dismissed her gloomy words. "They'll find it was a freak accident. Went up for a smoke, stone drunk, and slipped. Or leaned over to puke and lost his balance."

"You think so?" Louise forbore sharing her hypothesis about the railing height.

Tyler Quak paid no heed. A frown rippled across his forehead as he did a slow 180 to stare at the house and back at Louise. "You realize," he said, like someone with a novel idea, "if it wasn't an accident, it was the nephew. Marpel lost his cool when they argued. Cops tackle criminals all the time. Like in Jiu-Jitsu. Fling the old bully over."

"Tyler. We're not in the movies. The sergeant had plenty of time to cool down, even if their argument was heated. When Sgt. Marpel had tea up in our room after dinner, he was quite calm."

The young man's clenched jaw and fierce scowl told her he didn't like contradiction. His lips pressed tight in a childish sulk. Then he burst out, "Why is everyone on his side? Babette won't hear a word against him. Not even from Antonio."

"Goodness." Louise suppressed another eye roll. "Babette hardly qualifies as everyone. Of course, his godmother is also fond of him, but--"

"Fond?" Quak glared at her. "Babette loves him!" Her gaping astonishment acted as a further irritant. "Not like that. Like the son she never had." Consciously or not, Tyler slipped into imitating Babette's treble voice. "Goes on and on about how sweet he was as a kid and how kind he is."

In his own voice, he griped, "He got to spend all his summers here with her and his mom spoiling him."

"Oh? Natalie Marpel stayed, too?" It made sense for the two women to spend summers at the company's retreat. Louise suspected the place was mostly for private use but declared AEE property for tax purposes. It also divorced it from private assets.

"Yeah, sure. They kept the wives and the brat in style. The guys were too busy making money in the city." His face contorted in anger. "He had his mom and aunt all to himself during the holidays. My parents dumped me at camp and took off on grand tours. Every year!"

Wow, thought Louise, talk about displaced jealousy. In an icy tone, she pointed out, "Raymond lost both his parents at 14."

"Yeah, I heard. Not only once. Babs wanted to adopt him. But he blew it with his uncle. The moron refused to live with them and have anything to do with the AEE, ever." Quak's eyes sparkled with glee. "One bid the boss had no chance to win."

"Hence, Raymond Marpel had no reason to want his uncle dead. He avoided his uncle for decades."

"Yeah, but he's here now. Money doesn't stink. Inheriting is different from having to work for it."

"Hm...maybe." Louise left it vague.

"He's in for a surprise. The AEE isn't doing well. There's way too much competition now." A malicious smirk disformed Quak's attractive features. "The boss miscalculated. He was getting too old to run the show."

As she filed this interesting information for later consideration, Louise spotted Amita and Lilly bringing food to the patio. Drawn by her gaze, Quak turned to look.

"I'd better give them a hand," he said. "Might as well be useful."

"Good idea, Tyler. I'll let the vicar know about lunch."

No lunch invitation proved necessary. The vicar jogged toward her, teasing the dogs with a tennis ball to keep them close. Dr. Brown beamed at her, his scholarly face pink from the exercise.

"My, you have a way with dogs, Vicar. They adore you," she greeted him.

The vicar regarded Shadow and Spitz, who sat at his feet, tongues lolling sideways. His eyes twinkled when he proclaimed, "Little children, keep yourselves from idols." Straight-faced, he said to Louise, "Says the Lord, according to John."

He massaged the tennis ball between his pale hands. Chin raised toward the patio, he said, "Behold, the table is spread." With a boyish chuckle, he added, "Says I."

"Um, yes, so it is." Louise bent to stroke Shadow's head. The vicar's lighthearted mood in the wake of tragedy took her by surprise.

When she looked up, a somber expression met her.

"My lack of gravitas shocked you," he said. Turning to the bay, his hands swept outward as if to embrace the vista. "Even in the face of death, one cannot but marvel at the beauty of creation. A bright day dawns after the tempest. God's creatures come and go. Time ebbs and flows."

"Er, yes. True enough," Louise mumbled.

"Creation will remain in all its glory long after the last of us has passed. A comforting thought." He nodded to himself.

"Well, not if science is right and our solar system eventually goes the way of the wicket and implodes. Or explodes? Either way, it won't last forever."

This time, he nodded eagerly. "Change is part of the beauty."

"Um, yes. From an eternal perspective, we're just a blip on the face of the universe. A humbling thought." Louise mustered a smile. "Would you say that from that perspective it doesn't matter who sped our host on his way to eternity?"

"My dear Louise. Nothing of the sort." Shocked, the scholarly face peered up at her. "All life matters. 'Thou shalt not kill,' you know."

"Hmm, no more prosciutto for you, Vicar."

He chuckled with delight. "Shall we partake of the fruit of the earth, Louise?" With a gallant bow, he offered his arm.

Charmed by his old-fashioned courtesy, yet feeling rather sheepish, Louise accepted. A man, who had such command over playful dogs, must excel at leading his sheep. Hopefully not to the slaughter, she thought, smiling at her fanciful thoughts.

Chapter 18

For once, the luncheon spread held no attraction for Louise. Though the others hadn't returned to the patio yet, Tyler already urged Louise and the vicar to grab plates and serve themselves. They accepted only the offer of a cold drink.

Louise refilled the dog bowl under the outdoor tap and let the dogs find a shady spot to doze after their exuberant romp with the vicar.

"Babes in arms," murmured the irrepressible Dr. Brown, who strolled the length of the table, munching grapes. "In peace I lie down and fall asleep at once."

"Another quote, Vicar?" asked Louise with a smile.

"Psalms 4.8." He beamed at her.

From the armchair occupied by Antonio at yesterday's alfresco lunch, Tyler surveyed the food array. Hands resting on the corners of the chair, his arms stretched to full length, his pose struck Louise as proprietorial. Her mouth twitched in distaste. Lilly, who returned with a wine cooler, mirrored her reaction.

No love lost between those two, Louise thought.

From the patio door came Jenkins's hearty voice. "Perfect timing. Lunch is waiting for you, Mr. Gambit."

Hector ignored the comment and walked straight out onto the lawn, apparently aiming for the beach.

Jenkins pursed his lips as if to whistle but refrained. Instead, he turned to Amita. "Where's the lady of the house?"

The girl stopped fussing over the table arrangements. "Mrs. Arcadia went upstairs to her room, sir. Can I help with anything?"

"I was coming to that." Jenkins's face relaxed into a fatherly smile. "If the missus can spare you and Ms. Lilly, I'd like a word. Looks like the buffet is ready to roll." With a sweeping gesture at the display, "You sure brought it on."

Amita giggled. "Yes, lunch is ready. Can I go first?"

What a change from the girl's apprehension about police involvement, Louise mused. Still, the allure of regaling her friends and classmates with a first-hand account of a true crime would tempt not only teenagers.

The housekeeper ignored them all and left, with an empty tray tucked under her arm.

"Ms. Lilly. Don't go yet," called Jenkins.

To no effect. Lilly walked on.

"Lilly!" Tyler shouted. "The inspector wants you."

The woman spun around at an unprecedented speed. For the first time, Louise noticed a powerful streak in the angular features. Lilly's hazel-green irises must be ablaze, so fierce was the expression.

She certainly hissed like a snake. "Don't mess with me, Tyler Quak. You're not the boss here."

Tyler's 'not yet' sneer was unmistakable.

In her usual stoic tone, Lilly told Jenkins, "You can talk to me downstairs. I'm busy."

"So am I," said Jenkins, whose keen stare had followed the exchange. "I prefer the office. Come along, Ms. Lilly. You'll be next, Ms. Amita. Stay close."

Was the scalding glare Lilly shot Amita in passing a warning not to spy? Louise wondered. The request to be interviewed in the basement locale seemed intended to foil eavesdropping.

From Amita's pert smirk, Louise inferred the girl would recall urgent tasks in the pantry now.

At the patio door, Jenkins almost collided with Nora and apologized profusely.

"No harm done, Staff Sergeant." Mrs. Norton's hand fluttered in gracious dismissal. "Small people like me often escape notice." The tiny titter accompanying the words had Louise suspect the remark had a deeper meaning. "When will you interview me, I wonder?"

Jenkins became most affable. "No rush, Mrs. Norton. Enjoy your lunch in peace, and PC D'-Souza will take your statement later."

Rather than protesting at such cavalier treatment, as Louise had expected, Nora preened like the proverbial cat with one paw in the cream jug. Something was afoot.

This impression ripened into certainty when she observed Nora and Amita exchange a meaningful look.

"I'll get the coffee in a moment," the girl said and rearranged the table display for no apparent reason. Two minutes after Jenkins and Lilly departed, Amita rushed inside.

Sgt. Marpel, Louise assumed, remained on unofficial duty in the office, awaiting the next interview.

Mrs. Norton sidled up to Louise just as Wilma and Babette emerged from the house. The widow had changed into pearl-gray trousers and a plain, charcoal-colored top. Innocent of makeup, her face appeared subtly lined around mouth and eyes. She'd tidied her ponytail, now damp from a shower.

At her entry, Tyler jumped to attention, shedding his earlier brazen manner. He approached his late boss's wife diffidently.

When he arranged a chair for Babette, she said quietly, "Don't fuss, Tyler. I can manage," and turned her back on him.

His eager expression dissolved into a hurt, lost-puppy mien, the type Louise remembered from her canine's early days whenever she needed to crate the baby pooch.

The mental association reminded her to check on the dogs and found them snoozing side by side in their shady corner. The vicar truly tired them out. And himself. Dr. Brown held a siesta in a lawn chair. A plate heaped with food rested on a stool next to his chair.

"Psst," whispered Nora at Louise's elbow. "Let's grab our lunch and retire inside. Too much fresh air for one day."

Louise cocked an eyebrow at her friend and complied wordlessly. Since Nora picked merely a token amount of food, Louise figured eating wasn't at the top of their agenda. A bottle of water and a few bite-sized goodies wrapped in a napkin would suffice.

Nora chirped, "Babs? Louise and I will retreat inside for a while."

"Er, I'd better take Shadow," Louise said.

"Oh, leave him, please. They look so sweet to-gether." Babette's somber features relaxed into an adoring smile as she gazed at the sleeping dogs. "I'll keep watch while you take a break, Louise."

"Call me if he fusses," Louise said and followed Nora.

Once inside, Nora raised a finger to her lips and led the way upstairs. When they reached the first-floor level of the hexagonal staircase, Mrs. Norton didn't veer into the bedroom wing but handed her plate to Louise. Enjoining her again to silence, the genteel lady ducked under the yellow police tape, ignoring the bolded legend in all caps: DO NOT CROSS.

Louise suppressed her gut reaction that shouted, No go! Shamefaced, her mind admitted an urgent desire to inspect the scene of the crime. She handed over the plate and scrambled under the tape, fully aware that anyone might spot them from below on the open staircase.

At the top, the intrepid Mrs. Norton stepped onto the widow's walk. Mindful of her own tendency to vertigo, Louise put a cautious foot forward. With her back hugging the cupola's glass enclosure, she tested the wooden plank floor. To her relief, it had a steel substrate. Once black, the wrought-iron railing now blistered brownish-red rust. Exposure to harsh winters and storms had weathered its wooden top rail to a cracked gray-green.

When tiny Mrs. Norton rose on tippy toes to peer over the railing, Louise gasped. Even with the railing reaching Nora's chest, its corroded appearance didn't reassure.

"Come look," Nora whispered, excited by what she spied below.

Heart in her mouth, Louise gingerly stepped closer. Curiosity won the battle. She glanced down the sheer drop of the basalt cliff and swallowed painfully. No body. Did she imagine a faint chalk outline? Impossible to tell at such a distance.

Water lapped lazily onto the narrow ledge below. No beach. The cupola tower must be mounted directly onto the terraced cliff face. Her mind rapidly calculated the distance. Inside, the tower seemed a generous three-story height. Its rear dropped an additional 15 or 20 feet. Someone falling from this height stood an equal chance of landing in the water or on the crag's rocky outcrop.

A gentle tug at her sleeve diverted her attention to Nora, who pointed to the left below. By a freak of nature, a few spruces took root in crevices and grew up at crazy angles. In their shelter rested a policeman. Chin to chest, he either meditated or dozed in the afternoon shade. He didn't stir when, annoyed at their intrusion, a seagull screeched overhead.

When shifting her weight to scan the view to their right, Louise registered a tremor in the railing. Maybe it was her own body that trembled, she thought. Her teeth gnawed at her lower lip. Yet she persevered.

In any other situation, a panorama of this spirit-lifting beauty would elicit cries of awe and joy. Blues of sky and water merged at the horizon, where wispy cumulus clouds rose white and gray-rimmed into the heavens. Shafts of light danced on the rippling water.

Louise's gaze panned down to the shore. Beyond the lawn's perimeter, where she and Babette had walked the dogs, she spotted Gambit on the slope to the beach. From what she could tell, he took photos with his phone. Not of the bay but of the shoreline and the house. The red kayak still rested on the beach. Gambit made no move to escape.

"There's Hector," she murmured, not taking her eyes off the man.

A sense of movement and a dark shadow from above made her jerk back.

"What is it?" whispered Nora, who leaned forward at Louise's mention of Hector.

"Look." Louise pointed at the sky.

A bald eagle soared majestically, flapping its black-brown wings, then sailing gracefully. Head and tail showed white against sky-blue. It circled the cupola and descended onto a storm-ragged Jack pine. Only now, Louise recognized the impressive structure of branches and twigs at the tree's lofty height.

"The eagle roost," she murmured.

"They've always nested there," said Nora, unimpressed by nature's wonders. Bent over the railing as far as her petite figure allowed, Nora proved more interested in Gambit. Glee in her tone, she said, "I found out what he wrote."

"Nora!" The volume of her own exclamation had Louise shoot a glance at the almost forgotten constable among the spruce trees. He didn't move.

Lowering her voice, she said, "Don't tell me you raided his room." Then frowned. "I still have his printouts." Duplicates maybe.

"Heavens no." Mrs. Norton stood self-righteous and ramrod straight. "What do you take me for?" Smugly, she said, "Staff Sergeant Jenkins tightened the thumbscrews. Gambit came clean."

At Nora's reversion to her favorite noir crime lingo, Louise cracked a grin. The 'came clean' she judged hyperbole. Gambit probably stuck to headlines and bits and bytes. Still, Jenkins would insist on a copy.

Better not ask for details, or else Nora would expect reciprocal disclosures. To verify the means, she asked, "You were in the den?"

"Den?" Puzzled, Nora peered at her. "I was in the pantry. Amita told me they can hear every word from the office when they use a stepladder to get at the top shelves. I tried it for myself."

"Hm, yes, I saw it when I went through with the dogs. Didn't see a vent. The stuff on the shelf conceals it."

Nora's shoulders slumped. "Oh, you knew of it?"

Under different circumstances, the disappointment might be comical, Louise thought wryly. This wasn't a game of one-upmanship.

"I stumbled on Lilly in there," she admitted. "Plus, yesterday Amita and Lilly accused each other of spying when I heard them leave the pantry."

Her friend's lips twisted a little slyly.

"Nora? What plans are you hatching? It's not a game of Clue."

"No need for that stern look, Louise. It's you who's playing a lone game," Mrs. Norton aimed at a haughty stance. "Amita needs to fetch supplies for dinner preparation. If Jenkins interviews Lilly just then, so be it. The girl will go quietly about her business."

"Sooner or later, Jenkins will catch on."

"He'll haul us over the coals." Mrs. Norton tittered softly. "What else can we do when they don't share? Not even Raymond will tell me anything."

"Well, yes. Speaking of sharing, I talked to our Mr. Quak. Out in the open. No subterfuge." Louise grinned, then sobered. "Antonio suspected an affair between Tyler and Babette."

"Babs wouldn't." Nora's firmness brooked no dispute.

"Nor would Tyler," said Louise. "He wants to marry her. But she won't hear of it."

"Smart woman. He's weak. Can't trust him."

"Seems Antonio shared your opinion as he fired him. Tyler claims his boss would have retracted." Too late, Louise realized this was information from Tyler's interview. Not that her source mattered.

Bent again over the railing, Nora muttered, "I can't see it."

"What?" Louise leaned forward for a peek.

Nora peered up at her. "No. I mean, I can't see Tyler ever succeeding with Babs. If he thinks she'll be rich now, he'll be sorely disappointed. She's only got a settlement. Hank mentioned it when Antonio married her. So shabby of a husband to insist on a contract to protect his assets from his bride, I think."

"Goes both ways," said Louise. "In some cases, you wouldn't want the husband to gain access to the wife's property."

"True. It benefits Raymond and his family."

"You're sure Raymond is the heir?" Louise asked.

"No one else who could be." Yet, Nora frowned. "Antonio and Babs have no children, and his mother passed away years before Franco and Natalie's accident. He wasn't the type to leave his enterprise to some distant relative."

"Hm, with a man like Antonio, how can you be sure?" mused Louise. "There might be--"

"Watch out! It's not safe!" The shout cut off Louise and startled her and Nora enough to bump into each other.

Instinctively, Louise's arm flung around Nora's skinny torso and hauled her away from the railing.

Annoyed at overreacting, she stared at the housekeeper, who stood in the opening to the cupola's staircase.

Lilly stared back, saying, "You shouldn't be here. The police won't like it."

"Nor should you," Louise retorted. "And don't startle people."

"It's not good for one's heart," said Nora. Her hand flew to her chest in a dramatic gesture.

Lilly stood her ground. "It's my job to check what's going on in the house."

In her severe outfit, the angular features almost menacing when she scowled, the woman reminded Louise of teachers in black and white movies who punished minor misdemeanors mercilessly.

How long had the woman been standing there? Louise wondered and asked in a challenging tone, "Do you come up often to check?"

"I like to watch the eagles."

Lilly's unexpected admission eased the tension. Their faces swiveled to gaze at the nest.

There the eagle stood proudly surveying its domain. The head's white plumage contrasted sharply with the dark body. Louise recalled reading that the female of the species was larger than the male, though they had the same coloring. Unlike some other species, where the females appeared drab and camouflaged. Like cardinals or ducks. Like Lilly.

The unbidden thought struck Louise forcefully. Her eyes strayed to the housekeeper, who'd donned a slate-colored apron that further toned down the gray dress. Did the woman imitate nature and camouflage to discourage predators?

While Arcadia was alive, hiding the classic beauty, evident in the bone structure and in rare moments of animation, might have made him view her as a drudge beneath his notice. And his wife's notice...

What an idea. Louise's half-smile ceased when the implication sank in. Her ears tuned out of Nora's prattle about how the vista had matured since her last visit ages ago.

Was Lilly a scorned mistress who felled her lover in anger? No, that made little sense. Antonio suspected his wife of infidelity and sent the wife's alleged lover packing. The way he'd treated Babette the night before, and the veiled threats at dinner, augured no good for a marital future.

Lilly was most likely to stumble on Tyler chatting and joking with the boss's wife over the convenient vents. If she were Antonio's mistress, she would have ratted on them, but not disclosed how she obtained incriminating evidence.

At a fluttering and switching behind, Louise spun around.

"Oh, no!" she cried. "Not bats!"

"Bats in the belfry," a new voice mocked.

Chapter 19

The sight of Hector Gambit, framed by the cupola's glass enclosure, brought a blush to Louise's cheeks, ruing her fear of bats.

The boards creaking under his heavy footsteps as he joined them only increased her tension.

"Bats nest in the rafters," Lilly remarked. No admonishment for Gambit's violation of police barriers.

More immediate concerns crowded Louise's mind and made her stomach lurch. "Um, this thing looks too rickety to hold the four of us." If Gambit weren't between her and the safety of the stairwell, she'd have bolted right then.

Nora chuckled. "It's quite all right, Louise. I recall many a fine night when we tippled champagne under the stars. All seven of us." Her eyes grew misty. "Ginger ale for little Raymond."

The housekeeper turned her back on them and moved a step or two toward the front. Yet, Louise figured, the woman's ears remained peeled. Household duties apparently could wait. 'Nosy like the rest of us.' Louise's conscience pleaded guilty.

"You were a close friend of the family, Mrs. Norton?" asked Gambit.

"Oh, yes," said Nora. "My husband and I both were. I spent most time with Natalie and Raymond, of course."

Gambit nodded as if he'd expected that. "Were you here on the day of the Marpels' fatal accident?"

Someone must have set him straight about the accident's location, Louise mused, in which case Hector either must have disclosed his suspicions during the interview, or the mix-up had been a decoy.

Almost in a whisper, Nora answered, "No, Mr. Gambit. Not on that weekend." A tear formed and dislodged. She dabbed at it with the back of her hand, murmuring, "Excuse me."

"My apologies," said Gambit. "Shouldn't have brought it up if it's still painful to you. I just heard you reminiscing about the past..."

To Louise, such diffidence seemed uncharacteristic in a man like Hector, who probably tapped sources without qualms.

"The past bubbles up," Nora murmured. "It's Antonio's death. It all returns." The gray-blue eyes narrowed, and she peered up at the writer. In a firm tone, she challenged him. "What do you know about the accident, Mr. Gambit?"

He glanced into the distance. "Not much. The bare facts. Arcadia's brother and sister-in-law died due to brake failure on a steep descent. Their vehicle hit a tree. Both were pronounced dead at the scene."

It sounded like a practiced recital.

Mrs. Norton winced while he spoke. Now she whispered, "She was my dearest friend."

"I'm sorry for your loss." The standard phrase held no compassion.

To give him credit, Louise reflected, the accident dated back about 14 years.

"I understand Tony Arcadia and his wife followed in their own car. Tough to see it happen."

This was news to Louise. Did Gambit gain access to the police report on the accident?

"Tough does not capture losing loved ones," Mrs. Norton admonished him. "Raymond felt devastated at losing his parents." She, too, sought solace in the distant vista. A moment later, she said thoughtfully, "Babs wasn't ever the same after. She and Natalie were so close."

"So much worse to see it happen," murmured Gambit. "At least, she had you to share her sorrow and lean on."

Louise studied his face. Was there compassion beneath the sardonic veneer?

Nora sighed. "Babs never talked about it." She straightened and frowned. "You are quite adept at angling for information, Mr. Gambit. Maybe you'd like to reciprocate?"

Hector shrugged. His mouth twitched into a lop-sided grin as he leaned back against the frame of the glass enclosure.

"Now, I wonder," said Nora. "Why pick Antonio and his enterprise to write about, Mr. Gambit? He wasn't a big fish in the pond. Your book won't make a sensational splash."

"So much for confidence in my project. Can't say I blame you." He veered toward Louise. "Did you tell your friend what I wrote?"

"I did not," Louise said, quite offended.

"Believe me, Mr. Gambit, I tried. But she refused." Nora's titter made light of it.

Gambit probed further. "The sergeant then."

Such an idea was bound to offend the doting godmother. "My godson does no such thing."

Their exchange had caught Lilly's attention. Louise noticed her inching closer yet pretending to watch gulls sail in the breeze.

Loud shouting burst their conversational bubble. Startled gulls screeched in echo.

The commotion came from out front. Lilly hurried along the catwalk. In a languid movement,

Gambit pushed himself from the doorjamb's support and sauntered after the housekeeper. His gait suggested a mild interest, though Louise would bet he couldn't wait to see.

Mindful of her uneasy relationship with heights, Louise hugged close to the cupola's glass enclosure and followed Nora one gingerly step at a time. Mind over matter, she repeated her mantra, proud that she'd survived thus far without embarrassing herself.

Though the pitches varied, only one voice seemed to do all the shouting. Driven by curiosity, Louise inched forward to peer over Nora's head.

On the front terrace below, two constables blocked a tall man with a dark-colored turban from approaching the entry. The newcomer wore a tunic-like top, faded jeans, and work boots. His arms gesticulated as the officer closest to him spoke in a tone too low to reach the onlookers on the widow's walk.

Amita's father, Louise deduced. Come to retrieve his daughter.

A second later, her guess proved right when Amita rushed toward the man, calling, "Dad!

What are you doing here? We said five at the dock."

The father answered sharply in a language Louise didn't understand.

"What's going on here?" Jenkins crashed the scene, oozing authority in tone and stance.

The constables stood at attention, but their reply didn't carry up to the listeners.

Nor did Jenkins's words when he addressed the enraged father. Amita hung on to her dad's sleeve, entreating him to calm down.

"Come," Louise whispered into Nora's ear. "Let's leave."

They inched out of sight and then hurried to the stairway, leaving Gambit with the housekeeper.

When they reached the lower part of the stairs, Jenkins and a constable led Amita's father through the entrance hall. Presumably, the Staff proposed to interview the man.

As luck would have it, Jenkins caught sight of them. "There you are, Ms. Penfold. Stick around. You're next."

"Goodness." Louise mustered a demure expression. "That sounds ominous, Staff Jenkins. I'll be outside awaiting my turn." She rushed after Nora to the front terrace.

They found Amita arguing with the PC on guard duty. The officer sounded as though he'd repeated his "No, miss. It's not allowed" over and over.

"At least let me go explain. Dad just misunderstood which dock," Amita cried.

"That may be." The constable said, his face stoic, as if he'd heard it all. "Your father will tell the Staff."

His glance slid over Amita's head. He didn't seem pleased to see more women bearing down on him.

"Amita," Nora fluted. "Can we help?"

"Omigod, Mrs. Norton," cried the girl, whirling around. Dodging the PC, who attempted to block her, she rushed across the terrace. "Tell them I must be with Dad. He'll say––"

"Shhh, child," shushed Nora. "Not here."

"Come, Amita," Louise said. "We'll go around to the back. The constable won't mind. I need to check on my dog." She spared the man a polite nod and led the way.

Police communication must function flawlessly, Louise figured, when she spotted PC Lenner as soon as they circled the building's wing and emerged from the path.

"Please wait for your father outside," Lenner told Amita.

"It's so unfair." The girl almost stamped her foot.

Nora laid a soothing hand on Amita's arm and steered her toward the lawn.

"Did you see my dog?" Louise asked the constable. There was no sign of anyone else out.

"Mrs. Arcadia took the dogs with her inside," Lenner said. Her attention seemed directed at Amita and Nora.

Louise scanned the windows and spotted Babette in conversation with Raymond in the living room. With a jolt, she realized those two might discuss funeral arrangements. They were Antonio's closest relatives. There'd be a postmortem first. A sobering thought.

Just then, she saw Spitz and Shadow poking their noses at the patio door's glass. Before she could decide whether to let them come out, they'd run off again on business of their own. Better leave them with Babette.

"Coming, Louise?" called Nora. She lifted her hand in a gracious wave at PC Lenner. "Let us know when Amita's father is ready to leave, Constable." Not waiting for a response, Nora ushered them out onto the lawn.

They pulled their chairs close and huddled for a private talk.

"Now, Amita." Nora patted the girl's hand. "What is this all about? How did your father get here? And what might he say that worries you so?"

"Oh, Mrs. Norton. You don't know my dad. He fusses so." A deep sigh followed. "Dad never liked Mr. Arcadia." Then, brightly, "Mom says it's OK for me to do day shifts."

"Did you call or text? Telling your dad Mr. Arcadia died?" Louise asked.

"Omigod, no." Amita looked horrified. "I wouldn't ever."

"So, how did he find out?" Louise persisted.

Amita picked at the cuticles of her thumbnail and avoided Louise's gaze. "Stupid me told my younger brother. The airhead. He ratted on me to Gurpreet." A frown furrowed the flawless skin as Amita seemed to contemplate this chain of information transmission. "Gurpreet is the oldest. He's just like Dad."

"Well, no parent would want their daughter where someone was killed," said Louise.

"I guess not." Deflated, Amita's mouth puckered. Of a lively temperament, she perked up. "Oh, Mrs. Norton. I was in the pantry getting stuff when the inspector talked to Lilly." The girl looked pleased with herself.

"Were you indeed?" Nora said. "You couldn't help but overhear?"

Amita leaned close. "You won't tell Lilly I snooped?"

The dad's interview was receding into the background, Louise noted, hiding a smile.

"Heavens, no." Mrs. Norton assured their conspirator.

"It's so not true what Lilly told him." Amita's cheeks grew a shade darker, and her irises glowed. "Mean stuff about Tyler and Mrs. Arcadia. She's such a liar. Mrs. Arcadia would never. She's so nice."

From this convoluted speech, Louise inferred Lilly shared Antonio's view, which wouldn't be surprising if the housekeeper were his mistress. The question would be, who put the flea in whose ear?

Intrigued, Louise asked, "Did Lilly volunteer this--um--speculation?" When Amita's forehead creased, she reworded, "Did Staff Jenkins question Lilly about Mrs. Arcadia and Mr. Quak?"

As Nora nodded encouragement, the girl answered, "Yes, he did. Not straight out. He said, like, was the boss's wife and Tyler more friendly than you'd expect? And Lilly was like, Tyler says he loves her. I mean, Mrs. Arcadia. Which is so not true."

Curious, thought Louise, and asked, "Did Lilly claim Tyler admitted this?"

"Oh, no. Lilly heard him. And you know, Ms. Penfold, Lilly didn't tell the inspector she was spying on Tyler in the pantry. Else she wouldn't have heard him."

Louise and Nora exchanged a glance, and Louise murmured, "Well, it's understandable. You didn't mention the pantry to the staff sergeant. Or did you?"

A vigorous head shake was sufficient answer.

From afar, PC Lenner called, "Ms. Amita. You may leave now." In her somewhat lumbering gait, Lenner strode across the lawn.

Louise appreciated the officer's discretion in forewarning them of her approach.

Reluctant to depart, Amita fidgeted. Either she had more to share, or didn't relish the boat ride with her dad, Louise figured. The boat was interesting.

"How come Tyler picks you up when your dad has a boat?" she asked.

"Ah, no, we don't have a boat. Dad borrows our neighbor's sometimes."

Lenner was upon them now, and Amita slid from the chair like a cat unfolding gracefully.

More food for thought, Louise mused. So, the angry dad could reach the island unassisted. Hm, would he try by night during a tempestuous storm? No way. Nor with a house full of guests. There was no shred of evidence in the girl's behavior to suggest Antonio had ever harassed her.

"Your father is waiting." PC Lenner hooked her thumbs into the straps of the bulletproof vest. It lent her words marked authority when she told Louise, "Staff Jenkins would like to speak to you, Ms. Penfold. If you'd follow me."

Amita hugged Mrs. Norton and pumped Louise's hand. "Dad won't eat me," she told them. "He's really a pet most of the time."

The girl's light gait didn't speak of fear when she hurried ahead.

Into the lion's den, sighed Louise, and followed PC Lenner.

Chapter 20

Jenkins and his PC D'Souza already awaited them on the patio. Before they reached the officers, Louise caught Nora's attention. In a casual motion as if to stroke back her auburn hair, Louise cupped her ear and widened her eyes. Nora gave a quick nod.

Their underhanded exchange didn't escape the staff sergeant's vigilance. Louise doubted he understood the reference to eavesdroppers.

As D'Souza shepherded Mrs. Norton inside, Louise asked Jenkins, "Do you mind if we stay out here? It's so much pleasanter."

"Suits me fine," he said. "I won't mind stretching my legs for a bit."

By unspoken agreement, they walked toward the shore.

"Quite the place, isn't it?" said Jenkins. "Lucky devil who inherits it."

"Hm, yes," murmured Louise, noncommittal.

"Now, Ms. Penfold. The sergeant tells me you've been dabbling in crime." At her raised eyebrow, he smiled. "No offense, I'm sure you're good at what you do. So, let's pick your brains. You've poked around a bit. Come across any clues?"

"Goodness, Staff Sergeant. You don't need my input." The 'dabbling' still smarted.

"Don't be shy. Just speak your mind," he said, making things worse as far as Louise was concerned. Jenkins seemed to cotton on and changed his approach. "PC Lenner says you had long chats with Quak and Arcadia's widow. You and Mrs. Norton also dodged our tape. Inspected the scene of the crime, did you?"

At this, Louise blushed. How silly of them. Of course, the constable could see them from below. Wrongfooted, she opted for distraction. "We weren't the only ones."

"Mr. Gambit and the housekeeper joined you, I heard." He squinted at her. "Found anything interesting?"

Louise allowed herself a dismissive chuckle. "You and your team went over it already. Honestly, we assumed you'd finished up there."

A smug flicker twitched Jenkins's lip. "True. We are thorough." He tried another tack. "Gambit say anything interesting?"

"Like what?"

"Anything to do with Arcadia. Or what did you talk about?"

Under his relentless scrutiny, Louise had a hard time not squirming. She mustered a bland smile. "Nothing much. We talked about the eagle roost. Oh, and bats. And then we heard the shouting below."

"I see." He rubbed his nose. "Nothing else?"

"Well, Nora told us they used to go up there on starry nights. The three couples and Raymond when he was a kid. It made Hector ask about the accident. Er, not Antonio's death but the car accident that killed Raymond's parents. But you know all about that one," she added when he stared, unblinking.

"Curious," he said. "Word gets around, doesn't it? But it's true. I was a rookie on patrol that night. Nasty accident."

"Definitely an accident, though?"

"Now, what makes you say that, I wonder?" He eyed her intensely.

Her gaze panning the sprawling building and extensive property, she shrugged.

"Cui bono, eh? Boils down to that," he said, following her gaze.

"Well." Louise dragged the syllable beyond its natural length. "Not always. Or rather, it depends on the type of benefit involved. I guess if someone sets out to kill, they assume it will benefit them. Even if only relief from oppression, anger, or hatred."

Jenkins appeared more single-minded, asking, "Do the sergeant and his aunt inherit?"

"I couldn't say. Babette mentioned a settlement via marriage contract. Raymond would donate it to a women's shelter if he's the heir."

"Would he now?" Jenkins sounded unconvinced.

"I believed him. It cropped up in casual conversation while Antonio was still alive, and Mrs. Norton urged her godson to take an interest in the business." No need to mention that was only hours before Antonio died.

The staff sergeant whipped out his phone and thumbed its screen. His gaze fixed on the patio doors.

A moment later, Raymond came out. He wasn't fast enough in closing the door behind him. Shadow nosed past and, disregarding whatever Raymond said, raced to Louise.

"Good-looking fellow," Jenkins remarked as Louise bent to rub the pooch's head between her palms.

"Shall I leave you to have a word with the sergeant?" she asked and grabbed the dog's collar.

"Please stay. I may need your input. The sergeant won't mind." He nodded at Raymond, whose questioning look went from Jenkins to her.

"Staff?" Raymond's tone held inquiry and mild unease.

"Louise and I were wondering who inherits the lot. Is it you, Marpel?"

Being thus included, Louise didn't wonder Raymond frowned at her.

"As it stands, Tyler Quak," he told Jenkins.

"What?" cried Louise, only to apologize. "Gosh, I'm sorry. You took me by surprise."

"Man! And you didn't see fit to tell me earlier? That's a serious omission, Marpel." A furious red suffused Jenkins's neck and cheeks, leaving the peeling nose tip as a whitish beacon.

"You didn't ask me. Nor conducted a formal interview." Raymond stayed calm. Yet, Louise sensed he seethed below the surface.

"It's material information, Sergeant. I'd expect you to volunteer."

Uncomfortable with Raymond's dressing-down, Louise tried to ease the tension. "I assume this was news to you, too. Nora certainly doesn't know."

Jenkins's ire abated, just like the high facial color. "Tell us how and when you found out, Sergeant."

Raymond breathed deeply and let it out with a whoosh. His hand reached for Shadow's cranium and stroked the silky coat briefly. He straightened and, clenching his square jaw, addressed his OPP colleague. "Louise is right. My uncle told me yesterday. A bribe-threat combo, sort of."

Jenkins squinted so hard at Marpel he seemed almost cross-eyed to Louise.

Raymond continued, unfazed. "Remember, I told you he wanted me to leave the force and join the AEE? Making me his heir was the bribe."

"And the threat?" Jenkins's nose twitched like Shadow's when the pooch picked up an enticing scent.

"That Quak would remain his heir if I refused." Again, Raymond sighed. "I infuriated my uncle by saying that was fine with me."

"Ah," said Jenkins. If in doubt or in understanding was unclear to Louise.

"Jeez, I never met Quak until this weekend. I figured if he'd survived in my uncle's employment for years, he must really be capable and keen."

"Hm." The staff sergeant's calculating stare intensified. "Is our Mr. Quak aware of his good fortune, you think?"

"Good question. I asked my uncle if he'd told Quak. He laughed. Said he should be that stupid. Quak was a placeholder until I came to heel. So, no, I doubt Uncle Tony would ever tell him."

"No other threats?" asked Jenkins.

As Marpel hesitated, Louise sensed he was holding back.

"Out with it, man," Jenkins growled.

"Not a threat," said Raymond. "Uncle Tony grumbled about people's ungratefulness and leaving it all to a trust. Something big so his name would live on." Raymond shook his head. "I guess after firing Quak, he would have gone that route."

"Let me get this straight." Jenkins's forehead creased until his brows met in a bushy line. "Your uncle spoke to you when? And fired Quak at what time?"

"He ordered me to his office right after I arrived around 2 p.m. I was late for lunch. Not sure when he fired Quak. He announced it publicly at dinner."

"Ahem," Louise cleared her throat. "I can help with that. Not the exact time, but it was early afternoon. Between three and four, I'd say."

"Well, well," murmured Jenkins. Neither he nor Raymond asked where she got her information.

"I wonder where Tyler was when you and your uncle spoke in the office," she said to Raymond.

"All I can tell you, he was in the kitchen when I came out. He left right away."

"I see," said Louise. And literally saw with her mind's eye Babette grabbing Spitz at lunch and rushing inside after Antonio threatened to harm the dog. No question where Babette would seek refuge. The den was her safe place. She'd been in there until Louise came looking for a quiet spot to peruse Gambit's writing. Hence, Babette would have overheard Antonio arguing with Raymond.

Another image resurfaced. Tyler's face a mask of hatred, staring at Antonio when Babette fled with the Pom. He'd made to follow then but left the patio later while Louise and Gambit talked at the table. What's more likely than Tyler checking in with Babette? A young man in love with the boss's wife would not rest until he saw she was all right. It gave Tyler ample opportunity to hear firsthand of his good fortune. And of the possibility of losing it.

"Oh, my," she murmured.

Suddenly aware that neither man had spoken while she mulled this over, she looked up.

The staff sergeant's thumb and fingers rubbed his chin, creating a rasping sound. "You've remembered something."

"Um--er," stammered Louise. An irrational desire to protect Babette gripped her. If it were only Tyler, she'd own up, though she balked at disclosing her eavesdropping. What a mess she'd got herself into.

"Out with it." Jenkins stared hard, one eyebrow raised. "You know the law, Ms. Penfold."

Perhaps thinking her reluctance was personal, Raymond asked, "Should I leave?"

Louise's incisors gnawed at her lower lip. 'Don't turn coward,' her mind scolded. Straightening her spine, she spoke. "No. Please stay. Correct me if I'm wrong."

In a few words, she explained that Babette and Tyler could overhear Antonio arguing with Raymond.

Jenkins soon interrupted. "Let me get this straight. You're telling me anyone can hear what is said in Mr. Quak's office? And no one saw fit to warn me?" His face took on a crimson hue. "Marpel?" he bellowed.

Louise dug her nails into her palms not to cringe.

Bemused, Raymond knitted his brows. "I had no idea. Never been in the pantry. Nor the office until today. They didn't exist when I was a kid."

"The sergeant is right," said Louise. "The kitchen and cabinetry remodeling looks recent. Check with Babette. Anyway, it's hardly what matters here."

Deflated, Jenkins agreed. "Right. Let's have a go at Mr. Quak. Got lots of explaining to do. So has the lady of the house."

He yanked the tip of his nose between forefinger and thumb. Muttering, "We'll tackle her first," he strode to the patio.

When neither Raymond nor Louise moved, he called, "Coming? We haven't got all day. Show me the den you're on about," he added when Louise and Shadow caught up with him.

At the thought of facing Babette and owning up to her betrayal, Louise's stomach cramped.

'Nonsense,' her mind revolted. 'Who's betraying whom here?'

Chapter 21

As Jenkins sent Raymond in search of Babette, Louise perched on the edge of a living room sofa with Shadow by her feet. She watched the Staff summon two constables and position them inside the office and pantry. Though she couldn't hear his instructions, she assumed he ordered them to record whatever they heard and foil other eavesdroppers.

Minutes later, Raymond returned with Babette carrying Spitz.

"Good of you to spare me a moment, Mrs. Arcadia. May we use your room here?" Jenkins asked.

"Um, yes. If you wish." She tightened her grip because the Pom struggled against the embrace.

Over the widow's head, Jenkins squinted at Raymond and nodded when the other almost imperceptibly shook his head.

Louise took it to mean the sergeant had left his aunt in ignorance of what was coming. She could imagine Raymond's qualms in leading Babs into what must feel like a trap.

The staff sergeant's hand motioned for Babette to precede him. "Marpel, wait here for my instructions. Ms. Penfold? Please join us."

When she followed him with Shadow into the den, Louise noticed him panning the wall separating it from the office. He grabbed the desk chair and placed it below the vent.

Shadow made straight for the water bowl and slurped. The noisy splashing made Spitz whine for freedom.

"Let it go, Mrs. Arcadia," Jenkins said. "I'm used to mutts underfoot."

Bereft of the dog's comfort, Babette sat on the edge of the sofa, hands pressed between her knees. "What would you like to ask me, Mr. Jenkins?"

Disturbed by his looming over them and dominating the small room, Louise said, "Won't you sit, Staff?" She joined Babette on the two-seater.

Jenkins reached for the desk chair. It screeched under his weight. His thighs strained the fabric of his pants as he leaned forward and braced his broad palms on his knees.

He pinned the widow with narrowed eyes. "Who stands to gain?"

Both Babette and Louise winced at his blunt approach.

In a conversational tone, he said, "It's the first thing we ask ourselves in a case like this, Mrs. Arcadia. Usually, the wife and children inherit, or--"

"Not in this case, Sergeant," Babette interrupted. As if seeking support, she glanced at Louise. "My husband settled a certain amount on me at our marriage. It's modest by today's standards."

"So, I've heard," said Jenkins. "Any idea who gets the Arcadia enterprise?"

"You'll have to ask my husband's lawyers. Isn't that what the police do?"

"Not that simple, Mrs. Arcadia. Lawyers are cagey folks. Well, never mind that. Here's another thing. We're piecing together your husband's movements yesterday. I'm told you came in here for a bit of a rest after lunch. Is that correct?"

"Umm, yes. Spitz and I took a quick break."

Ears pricked, the Pom stopped worrying a stuffed toy and leapt onto the sofa to nestle between the women.

"Meanwhile, your husband talked to your nephew." Jenkins rose, thus towering over them.

Spitz sat up. With her black button eyes on the man, her upper lip curled to expose her sharp canines.

Louise readied to grab the Pom's collar.

Staff Jenkins coughed and said louder than necessary, "Excuse me."

From next door floated a female voice over the vent. "Is that you, Staff? I'm in the office, looking for you."

PC Lenner was a lousy actress, thought Louise. It wouldn't fool even the unsuspecting Babette.

"Well, well," muttered Jenkins. "I'll be damned--excuse me, ladies." Facing the vent, he hollered, "Stay put, Lenner. Be with you soon."

"Righto, Staff," they heard the constable confirm.

Satisfied with his show, Jenkins sank onto the chair. A smug expression flittered over his features, immediately replaced by bland affability.

He picked up the conversational thread. "Let's see. While your husband discussed onboarding with your nephew, you and the pooch snuggled up in this cozy spot. You heard Marpel refuse to have any truck with his uncle's business."

Louise leaned sideways against the sofa's armrest and stole another glance at her neighbor.

Babette said nothing. Her fingers squeezed her skinny legs, pink nails digging in. Alert to the tension, Spitz nudged her arm, but to no avail.

Jenkins watched. Though he had his face under control, Louise observed his hawk-like eyes glittering.

His index finger jabbed toward the vent. "It got noisy next door. No one in here could help over-hear what was said. Isn't that so, Mrs. Arcadia?"

Recalling her earlier talk by the shore, Louise expected a denial rather than Babette's whispered, "I might have heard a word or two." The earbuds would have been the obvious copout.

Jenkins pounced on the admission. "Like Mr. Quak being the heir? Eh? That word would stick out a mile."

When Babette winced as if struck, he piled on more. "Here's the rub. Your husband took against Quak and threatened to leave the whole show to a trust in his own name. Quite a blow to Mr. Quak, wasn't it? I bet it stunned him when he heard."

Wow, thought Louise, he really knows how to land a blow himself.

In a crisis, Babette's acting skills seemed to desert her, because she stared wide-eyed at the officer. Tears trickled over the sculpted cheek-bones. The skin appeared pale beneath the tan.

Impulsively, Louise's hand reached to comfort but stopped midway, unsure if she'd make matters worse. A nagging worry intruded. Was she double-fooled and fell for an act?

Unfazed by the interviewee's distress, Jenkins thumbed his phone, saying, "We'll ask the man himself."

No one spoke while they waited. Spasmodic sniffles from Babette, who again clutched the white dog close to her chest, taxed Louise's self-restraint.

Louise's palm reached to cup the top of Shadow's head when he hugged close to her knees. Dogs sensed human emotions better than humans themselves, she thought. And they provided solace unstintingly.

A familiar metallic sound intruded into her reverie. The staff sergeant stood by the door and tapped its knob with something in his fingers. A coin or other metal object, she figured. What an annoying habit.

He stopped when a sharp rap on the door announced the man they were waiting for.

"Ah, Mr. Quak. Good of you to come." The jovial greeting fooled no one. After letting Tyler pass,

Jenkins stuck his head out the door, saying, "I'll text if I need you, Sergeant."

Still hugging Spitz, Babette jumped to her feet, her tearstained face in turmoil.

Louise inched to the edge of the sofa, readying to leave.

Focused solely on Jenkins, Tyler said, "Pleased to oblige." His mouth stretched into a mechanical smile.

"Oh, Tyler!" Whatever Babette's tragic outcry conveyed remained anyone's guess.

Quak took one step toward his late boss's wife, then whirled around to face Jenkins. "What have you done to her? What's going on here?"

His furious stare shifted to Louise. "Is this your doing?"

Conscious of some truth in his accusation, Louise said nothing.

"Now, hold on, Mr. Quak. This is still my show." Jenkins's authoritative voice restored order. "Sit yourself on that chair there. Mrs. Arcadia, you and your little pooch can take a break."

He opened the door, calling, "Marpel! Get your aunt some tea."

For a moment, it seemed Babette might refuse. Perhaps accustomed to subservience, she left in silence.

When Louise rose to follow, he stalled her. "Stay put, Ms. Penfold." He shut the door and leaned against it.

Across from Louise, Tyler opened his mouth as if to protest. Then shut it like a clap. He leaned forward, wide-legged, and clasped his hands loosely at knee level.

"What's this about, Jenkins? If you've given Mrs. Arcadia the third degree, you'll hear from the Arcadia lawyers. She just lost her husband. Don't you have any decency?"

Beneath the bluster, Louise sensed frantic calculation. His nervous hand forked back the sunbleached hair.

Idly, she wondered about his salary as Antonio's assistant to afford high-end clothing. As the heir, he could indulge in more than classy outfits if he resurrected the AEE to its former glory.

In no hurry to respond, Jenkins took a stand that put both Quak and Louise in his purview.

He let Tyler stew for another minute before saying, "This is a police investigation. Our aim is the truth. You, Mr. Quak, were less than truthful."

Under Jenkins's scrutiny, mightier men might quail, mused Louise. Quak writhed in his chair.

"I didn't lie to you." Tyler's quaking tone did his name honor.

"That remains to be seen. You didn't correct my mistaken assumption that Mrs. Arcadia inherits everything. Most common for the wife to get it all where no kiddies are involved."

The natural color returned to Tyler's face. His voice steady again, he said, "You can't expect me to know the terms of my boss's will. Ask Mrs. Arcadia. Or your sidekick, Marpel, should have told you."

"He did." Jenkins took a step closer and did his squinting act. "It's you, Mr. Quak, who's the lucky heir."

"Me?" Tyler broke into a high-pitched laugh. "You're kidding." The renewed laughter ended in a coughing fit.

Except for the artificial undertone, the reaction might have convinced, Louise reckoned. Judging by his expressionless stare, the investigator didn't buy the performance.

As no response came, Tyler sobered. "You're having me on."

"Not at all, Mr. Quak. Don't pretend it's news to you. Heard it straight from the horse's mouth yesterday after lunch. You and Mrs. Arcadia were right here, I'm told. You wouldn't contradict a lady now, would you?"

Smart move to insinuate Babette had owned up. Louise applauded the investigator's skill. Put on the spot, he could truthfully claim the lady in question was Louise, who'd shared her inference.

Tyler fell for it. "I just dropped in for a moment to ask her about--about barbecuing for dinner."

"And the two of you overheard Mr. Arcadia's little spat with the nephew next door. What luck he named you as his heir." Jenkins scowled menacingly. "Then, with a casual word or two about a trust fund, he spirited it all away again. Was it that final taunt that had you sneak after him to the cupola last night and push him over?"

"I didn't kill him!"

The anguished cry reverberated in the tiny room and made Shadow jump to his feet, ruff raised on his neck. His lip curled in a warning snarl.

Louise's fist closed around the dog's collar. On her sharp, "Sit!" he sank back onto his haunches but remained on high alert.

"PC Lenner! You and D'Souza get over here." At normal volume, Jenkins told the shaken Quak, "We'll continue this at the station."

A moment later, the room seemed to swarm with people, though only two had entered.

Her eyes on Tyler, Louise half listened to Jenkins's thanks for her cooperation.

Wedged between the uniformed officers, Tyler craned his neck to seek Louise. He pleaded with her. "You've got to believe me. I didn't kill him."

The ashen grimace of despair was the last she saw of Tyler Quak.

Chapter 22

Tyler's face still haunted Louise when she took the dogs for a pre-dinner run through the woods a few hours later. Ignorant of human affairs, Spitz and Shadow dashed in and out of the ferns lining the trail. Their noses to the ground, the canines pursued enticing scents, magnified by a light mist before sundown.

Though Louise's eyes remained watchful, her mind rambled, torn by conflicting emotions. Too many open questions and loose threads for the police's departure with Tyler to be a satisfying end.

True, Jenkins hadn't formally charged Tyler Quak. He'd told Babette that Mr. Quak was assisting the police in their inquiries. No one was fooled.

That Babette didn't break down in tears when Jenkins denied her request to speak to Quak was a relief. She'd requested the Staff to let Tyler know she would arrange for a legal representative.

Shortly after, Raymond had taken the boat to ferry the Browns to the mainland dock. Despite Wilma's assurance she'd be in touch after the weekend, Louise had sensed a marked coolness toward Babette. Presumably, donors would abhor bad press about Mrs. Arcadia's AEE connection and murder. Or would they? Louise mused with a touch of cynicism. After all, the fundraising was for theatrics. Live drama might appeal.

Any warmth lacking in Mrs. Brown's goodbyes, the vicar supplied with dividends, seasoned with words of wisdom, enjoining hope and strength. The dogs received their fair share of clerical kindness. They, like Louise, recognized the fun-loving boy in the scholarly man of God and had enjoyed his company.

Neither Gambit nor Lilly was in evidence to see off the police party or the Browns. Without Amita's help, the housekeeper would be busy in the kitchen or tidying guest rooms.

Hector's self-effacement puzzled Louise. Tyler's removal ought to be grist to his mill. Raymond and Nora--and by extension, Louise--staying on to support the widow was only natural. Gambit's continued presence, even if behind the scenes, appeared intrusive. More unfinished business.

To give Babette, Nora, and Raymond space for a family huddle, Louise opted for walking the dogs, savoring the stillness of the serene woods. Nature was never silent, Louise mused, as evening birdsong floated on the breeze. Twigs crackled underfoot. Chipmunks squeaked. The dogs panted and rustled through the undergrowth, rushing to and fro.

The mellow pre-sunset atmosphere soothed the mind. So, why the anxious undertow? The crime was solved. The criminal apprehended. Impatient with herself, Louise shook her head and called the dogs. Time to head back and face the ordeal of a postmortem dinner.

Back at the house, Louise fed the dogs and had a quick shower before going down to dinner. Much to the housekeeper's disapproval, Babette insisted the dogs would be fine having the run of the house. She'd left the den door open, and Spitz raced in and out fetching dog toys. To calm both dogs, Louise gave each a hard yak milk bone. It would keep them busy throughout dinnertime.

Babette ushered her guests to the dining table in front of the grand windows. Louise didn't mind sitting with her back to the outdoors. Darkness had descended. Except for the dimmed outdoor lighting on the patio, nothing was discernible. The bay was a distant memory.

She sat next to their hostess, with Nora on Babette's other side. Louise offered to help Lilly bring up the food from the basement kitchen but received a curt rejection. Raymond jumped into the breach and was wordlessly accepted.

Across from Louise lounged Hector Gambit, his face a study of ease. Yet, beneath the mask, she sensed high alertness. He'd sauntered in last minute, apologizing for his absence during the afternoon. "When the muse strikes, one must obey," he said with practiced self-mockery.

The place at the head end of the table remained conspicuously vacant.

When Raymond and the housekeeper placed steaming bowls of pasta, roasted autumn vegetables, meat, and fish dishes on the table, Babette said, "Ray, would you grab a place setting for Lilly from the sideboard, please?"

Lilly gave her employer a sullen look, saying, "I've got things to do."

"You need to eat like the rest of us and worked double as hard today without Amita to help with chores," said Babette. "Toss your apron somewhere and have a glass of wine. You deserve it."

Raymond pulled a chair into the space between Gambit and his own and placed a dinner set for the housekeeper. Louise thought it awkward for the housekeeper to face her employer throughout dinner. But seating her at the foot or head end of the table would have been a worse move.

The housekeeper had left the room but returned minutes later minus the apron and headscarf, the dark hair rolled into a tight bun at the nape. Such a severe hairstyle increased the angular features. Louise caught a glimpse of the striking hazel eyes before Lilly sat down with awkward reluctance.

Like herself, Louise noticed Gambit covertly observing his table neighbor. His attention seemed absorbed by the wineglass he held up at arm's length as if it warranted inspection. The sidelong glances he darted to his left betrayed his interest.

For the next few minutes, table talk languished. Praise of the truly delicious food received no reaction from the housekeeper. Polite murmurs, offering the various dishes to each other, dissolved in the jingle of cutlery on porcelain and tinkling glass.

Into the desultory mood, Gambit said, "You've got an impressive place here, Mrs. Arcadia. Will you keep it?"

Their hostess lowered her wineglass and regarded her guest across the table. "It is not for me to keep. It goes with the Arcadia Enterprise."

Gambit raised a sardonic eyebrow at Raymond and drawled, "Lucky devil."

No one set him straight on inheritance matters.

When Raymond ignored him and Louise resorted to an innocuous remark about tomorrow's weather, the writer probed further. "At least, you've got a nice place to live in Toronto."

"The condo is also company property," Babette said, and turned to offer Nora more vegetables.

Oh, dear, thought Louise, Antonio's lawyers really took young Babette for a ride when they deprived her of the right to the matrimonial home.

"So where will you go?" asked the irrepressible writer.

"I don't think my aunt's plans are any of your business, Gambit," Raymond said, not bothering to look at the man.

"It's okay, Ray," Babette spoke quietly. Rather than answering Gambit, she addressed the housekeeper. "I'm sorry, Lilly. I meant for us to discuss this privately. You must be wondering." She waited for the woman across from her to react.

It took a moment before the housekeeper glanced up wordlessly from the food on her plate. Her right hand clenched around the fork. She'd hardly eaten anything, Louise noticed, but assumed the woman snacked while cooking.

"We'll have time to talk in Toronto, but just to let you know. After my husband's funeral, I'll go home to my people. We'll make some arrangements for you to get two extra months of vacation pay to tide you over. Nora and I can help you find a new position quickly."

A generous bonus by the usual standards for domestic employment. Louise reckoned that labor law entitled Lilly merely to a two-week notice and vacation arrears.

When the housekeeper nodded and stabbed at a chunk of meat on her plate, Babette turned to Louise. "My brother still works the family farm in New Brunswick. It's right by the sea. I haven't been back." Her gaze misted over.

Louise sensed there was another story here. Had the family disapproved of Babette's marriage and lifestyle? Or Antonio of Babette's farming folks? Not likely with his own humble origins.

To spare Babette, and to spite Gambit, whose ears were pricked despite the bored expression, she didn't ask for details. "That'll be a wholesome break now. A farm by the sea is so serene."

Not during the stormy winter months ahead, her mind commented.

The yearning in the blue eyes told her that no prospect of storms, emotional or environmental, could mar Babette's desire for a homecoming.

"Nora, you, and Shadow must visit next summer," Babette murmured. "Raymond and his family will come too."

When Louise thanked for the invitation, relieved that the widow planned a future rather than despairing about the present, she caught the housekeeper's scowl. Surely, there wasn't much to envy in moving to a remote farm.

In a sudden change of topic, Babette addressed the writer. "Mr. Gambit? Louise mentioned you had some old photos of my husband. May I see them before you leave?"

At that, Gambit's head shot up. He stared at her for a moment. A slow grin widened his mouth. His hands patted his pockets and withdrew a mobile. Despite Babette's "Oh, not now," his thumbs scrolled. He pushed the device across to Louise.

She checked the screen. As expected, it displayed Babette's younger self, perched on a punter's lap at a bar, with Antonio leering next to them. Louise's anger rose. How cruel to confront the widow with her past now. But when she made to hand back the device, Babette reached for it with a polite, "May I?"

One glance at the image and Babette blushed fiercely. She pushed the phone to Louise as if it burned her fingers.

A movement across the table drew Louise's attention to the housekeeper. Astounded, she saw a smile flicker across the woman's stoic features. It vanished when the woman's gaze dropped to the phone in Louise's hand.

Raymond sat, his jaw clenched, but he did not interfere. He'd have a go at Gambit after dinner, Louise could bet.

She shot a quick glance at Gambit. Engrossed in watching Babette's reaction, he made no move to get his phone back.

Louise swiped through the images. In seconds, she found what she was looking for. Her ears took in Nora whispering to Babette. But her eyes and mind studied the enlarged excerpt of a young woman's photo. Louise scrutinized the features, the prominent forehead, black curls, crowned by the feather diadem.

Sensing Gambit's focus shifting to her, she stared back. His supercilious smile wavered when she didn't speak. A trace of impatience crept into his tone. "And? Do I get it back?"

Louise held the phone beyond Hector's reach, its screen facing him. She'd raised her voice to draw attention.

"It's your mother, isn't it, Mr. Gambit?"

Chapter 23

Though worded as a question, Louise never doubted the woman in the photo was Gambit's mother. The resemblance was too strong. And it all fit so well.

As everyone stared at him, Gambit's outstretched hand no longer aimed to grab the phone but shifted a wine bottle by an inch.

She repeated, "It's your mother."

Anger flickered in his eyes. Yet his tone mocked. "What if it is?"

"Yours is not a dispassionate interest in the adult entertainment industry as you'd like your readers to believe. It's deeply personal."

"What if it is?" he repeated.

"She is your primary source on Antonio, isn't she?" Louise said.

Babette's slim hand reached over. "May I see?" A spark of interest animated her voice. "Maybe I knew your mother, Mr. Gambit."

"Not likely," he drawled. "Your husband discarded her long before you joined the club."

"Babs? Hadn't you better wait?" Raymond no longer held back.

Louise assumed he meant wait and talk this over first, preferably with the lawyers.

His aunt didn't heed the caution. "No. I never met her," she said, handing the phone to Louise. It sounded almost regretful. "There's nothing shameful about being a working girl, Mr. Gambit," she said.

Maybe the stress of this horrid day warped Babette's judgment, because she confided in her housekeeper, who listened with an inscrutable expression. "You'd never guess, Lilly. I worked for my husband before our marriage."

Raymond intervened. "Babs, really, I don't think we should--"

Gambit's strong voice cut in. "You were the lucky one, Babette. Played your cards right."

A gasp from Nora and Raymond's "That's enough, Gambit" met the implied insult.

"It was intended as a compliment, Marpel. Your aunt was just smarter than all of Tony's girls back then." He doffed an imaginary hat at his hostess.

Louise looked across at Raymond and Lilly's faces, both scowling now. Her fingers swiped back to the grainy polaroid copy she'd seen first yesterday afternoon. The one of a drunk young Antonio with the frightened, yet seductive waif.

She raised the phone toward Lilly without relinquishing her hold.

"Your mother worked for Antonio too. Didn't she, Lilly?" Louise observed the woman blanch, then turn an ugly crimson.

Leaning forward in her seat, Louise offered her the phone. Lilly's hand reached but pulled back in reflex as if too close to a hot stove.

With a frown, Raymond murmured, "Let me see, please," and took the phone from Louise's fingers. For a moment, no one spoke. Manners in abeyance, they all stared at Raymond, scrutinizing the housekeeper's face. He passed the phone back to Louise instead of Gambit.

Lilly shrunk back in her seat.

This time, Babette sounded far weaker as she murmured, "There's nothing shameful about dancing."

Gambit, of course, had figured it out, too. His gaze struck Louise as compassionate when he said to Lilly, "Your mother met him in Quebec when she worked at a motel lounge. He took her to Toronto. Used her and dropped her, just like my mom. I hope she managed better than mine."

Thoroughly frantic now, Lilly's hazel eyes darted from Gambit to Raymond, who leaned closer, asking, "What happened to your mother, Gambit, that made you so bitter?" There was genuine interest in his question.

Gambit laughed his cynical laugh. "Couldn't cope. An overdose. Like you, I was orphaned young. Only difference, no posh home for me."

He laughed again. "Hey, what am I saying? My foster mom wasn't half bad."

"I'm sorry," said Raymond. "Your dad--"

"Never met him," Gambit said. "Some punter she had a fling with. Doesn't matter. I forged my destiny, man."

Raymond nodded. It seemed to Louise his acrimony toward Hector dissolved.

Wedged between the two men, the housekeeper inched her chair back. Not to clear the table but to jump up and leave.

"Lilly?" Louise said softly. "Is that what happened to your mom?"

"I don't know what you're talking about," Lilly snapped.

"An overdose, I mean. I know your father wasn't one of the punters."

Next to her, Babette breathed in sharply. "Really, Louise--"

"What do you know about my father?" hissed Lilly. "It's none of your business."

"Antonio Arcadia was your father, wasn't he, Lilly?" Louise said.

Stunned, Raymond swung around in his seat to face Lilly's profile.

The woman clenched her square jaw but said nothing.

Nora leaned forward. Peering at the housekeeper's face, she announced, "Yes, I do see the resemblance. The Arcadia chin. And the bone structure. Just like Antonio. You have it too, Raymond." She studied the woman closer. "The high cheekbones, eyes, and hair come from your mom's side, I guess. Is that what tipped you off, Louise?"

Thoroughly uncomfortable with Nora's dissection of the woman's looks, yet knowing worse was to come, Louise nodded.

Beside her, Babette appeared in shock. At Nora's eager, "Don't you see it, Babs?" Antonio's widow rallied. She stretched out both hands, exclaiming, "Why didn't you tell us, Lilly? Why come like a stranger and work for your own father?"

As if in sudden realization, Babette's hands flew back and crossed below her collarbone. Her cheeks flushed, she whispered, "He treated you very badly--I'm so sorry."

Stung, Lilly jumped up, her chair toppling backward. "My father?" she cried. "That man fathered me. He was no father. The creep used her and spat her out when she got pregnant. Not even 17 and on the streets. Alone."

The breathless vehemence of the accusations held the others spellbound.

"I'm so sorry," murmured Babette. "Your mom's folks wouldn't have her back." It wasn't a question. Louise suspected Babette's people had washed their hands of her too, when she became a dancer of the less reputable kind.

Raymond rose quietly. "Sit down, Lilly," he said. As a cop, he'd see the implication, Louise figured. She noticed a phone in his hand and assumed he had activated recording.

"Did he know she was with child?" Nora asked. "Even Antonio wouldn't--"

"Of course, he knew." Lilly spat the words. "I found his letter in the stuff she left behind when she took off. She'd folded it around a photo of him, his name scribbled on the back. The filthy swine said she'd never know who fathered her child the way she carried on. Only she swore she didn't."

"They had paternity tests when you were a child," Nora said. "She could have proven it."

Gambit's cynical chuckle interrupted. "Let's assume Lilly's mother didn't have the means for a lawyer and a court case. Arcadia had money and clout."

Though Louise doubted Antonio had either back in those days, she realized the courts in the 1980s would have given little credence to a minor of ill repute, as they would see it. She imagined Antonio gave the girl a small sum and sent her packing.

As Lilly sank back onto the chair, Louise said, "You mentioned your mother took off. Did she leave you with relatives?" The alternative was horrible to contemplate.

An ugly sound, a cross between a guffaw and a sob, broke from Lilly's lips. "She left me all right. In the dump we shared with a dozen other squatters. One of them took me and a bundle of our stuff to social services and ran. I was eight. Foster homes for me until I went on my own."

"Kudos to you," said Gambit with obvious fellow feeling. "You've come a long way."

Had she really? thought Louise. It seemed to her, Lilly had come full circle. Or never left.

Aloud, she said, "You told him last night, didn't you, Lilly? Up on the widow's walk?"

Babette gasped. Raymond went on high alert. He still hovered next to Lilly's chair.

Lilly stared at her accuser, mesmerized.

"But why wait this long?" asked Nora. "Lilly has been working for the Arcadias for a few months. Babs, didn't you say you got a new housekeeper through an agency last spring?"

Mechanically, Babette nodded, not taking her eyes off the housekeeper.

"Why last night, Lilly?" persisted Nora.

"I think I can tell you that," Louise said when Lilly clenched her fists and remained mute. "Lilly overheard Antonio telling Raymond about changing his will. I imagine that was the ultimate insult to his daughter." She didn't want to spell it out in front of Gambit. "Did you hope finding out he had a child would have changed his mind, Lilly?" A vain hope, if so.

"He so wanted a boy," said Babette. "Now I know why he was sure it was my fault we never had children. The doctors agreed with him."

Lilly broke into hysterical laughter. Almost choking on the words, she cried, "A boy. He wanted a boy. Not me."

"Is that what he told you last night?" asked Louise. "Up there on the widow's walk?"

The laughter morphed into a shriek. Sobering, she said, "I'd waited on the landing to speak to him. He was half-drunk and went to the top for a smoke. All I wanted was a job with the AEE to prove myself. Be his assistant."

"You figured you would earn his respect in the business. Later, when he trusted you, you'd tell him who you are," said Louise. A plan bound to go awry, given Antonio's character.

Lilly nodded as if grateful for being understood. "I knew I could do Tyler's job, I told him." The woman's features contracted in ill-suppressed fury. "He laughed! Tried to grope me. That's when I told him who I was." She shuddered.

Her hazel eyes ablaze, she added, "He killed himself laughing."

"Literally," remarked Louise. "Laughing, he probably leaned back against the railing, and you grabbed his legs and flung him over."

Babette cried out in horror.

"Sorry, Babette. I had to be blunt," said Louise.

"Heavens, you killed your own father," cried Nora.

"He wasn't much of a father," Gambit remarked.

Hector must love getting a sensational story handed to him, Louise reckoned. The story of his life.

This time, Lilly jumped to her feet so quickly, it left Raymond gaping.

They hadn't reckoned on the woman's speed. In one swift move, she sped into the living room.

Awakened by the commotion, the dogs raced after her, Spitz yipping at the top of her voice and Shadow providing a bass drumbeat. Dumbfounded, it took Raymond a moment to sprint in their wake. Louise hastened after them.

Inside the cupola's main floor, Lilly aimed for the front door. A futile move, as the woman stood no chance of leaving by boat. The dogs mistook it as a signal for their nighttime pit stop. They stood blocking the front door, waiting to be leashed.

Wild-eyed, the woman turned and dashed up the stairs, regardless of Raymond's, "Stop! Lilly!"

He made a move to chase her, but she kicked back and almost connected with his head.

Mindful of the escalating danger, Louise followed behind. The dogs scented a fun chase. They raced past her and jumped around the fleeing woman. Lilly kicked at the yapping hounds and connected with Spitz's rump. The Pom yelped shrilly. Baffled, Shadow stopped to check in with his buddy.

From below came Babette's shriek, "Don't hurt her!"

It was clear to Louise the concern was for the dog, not the patricide.

Raymond proceeded more cautiously now. Presumably, he figured he stood a better chance at the top.

Shadow had no such inhibitions. Perhaps re-membering a previous chase, he leapt after Lilly. Just on the last steps before she reached the opening onto the widow's walk, the tall dog jumped against her back from behind and brought her down flat. Arms flung out, the house-keeper crashed face forward onto the wooden boards, her torso out while her feet were still on the last steps.

It took Raymond seconds to pull her up, arms pinned to the back.

"Lilly Mallory, I arrest you for the unlawful killing of Antonio Arcadia––"

The rest went under in Lilly's shriek and Gam-bit's shout from a few steps behind Louise, "You can't do that, Marpel. You're not on duty."

"You bet I can," said the sergeant. "Don't inter-fere, Gambit."

A little breathless from the adrenaline rush, he turned to Shadow. "Great job, bud. You can join the force." He spared a smile for Louise, saying, "You go first. We'll follow. Double treat for Shadow tonight."

Chapter 24

Early afternoon the next day, the three women and their dogs embarked on the road trip back home in Louise's car.

"You're sure you won't mind the detour?" Louise asked Babette in the backseat with a dog on each side. In the car's interior rearview mirror, the widow's face looked fatigued despite discreet makeup and styled dark curls.

With Nora and Babette, plus the two dogs, the hatchback felt cramped. Babette had refused to drive Antonio's luxury SUV--ever again, she'd said--and Raymond went a different route to meet his wife and baby daughter at his in-laws.

He took some of the luggage and promised to drop it off the next day in Toronto.

"I'll be okay," Babette said now. "It's time to lay the ghosts. I'm more worried about you, Nora." Her slender hand reached between the front seats and rested for a moment on Mrs. Norton's shoulder.

"I'm all right," Nora said. Though from the corner of her eye, Louise saw Nora's nervous fingers cramp on the handbag they clutched. "Hank and I visited the site after the funeral back then." Her face turned towards Louise in the driver's seat. "I just felt I had to lay flowers where Natalie died."

Louise had programmed the route to the lookout, high above Georgian Bay, in Maps and followed the directions that crisscrossed the hinterland. They'd parted with Raymond on the mainland dock. A local caretaker would berth the boat, and with his wife's aid, close up the house once the police completed their investigation.

None of them would want to stay at Eagle Roost when they returned for the inquest. There were lots of hotels and resorts along the shores and in town if they chose to stay overnight. Such a shame, though, thought Louise. The island residence was a magnificent place. A place forever marred by the memory of death.

What an irony of fate! How Antonio must turn in his grave to see the man he suspected of being his wife's lover inherit it all! Er, Louise's mind corrected itself. He's not there yet. If all went well, Arcadia's interment would go ahead in another week. Probate would take far longer. What happened to the AEE in the meantime was anyone's guess. It depended on its executive's chain of command. Tyler Quak would know how to get control, she reckoned.

Aloud, she said, "Did they let Tyler go last night? Do you know, Babette?"

"They did. He texted me around midnight." Babette leaned sideways, presumably to see Louise's profile. It put her outside the line of the rearview mirror's vision. "I never believed Tyler harmed Antonio. I was sure he didn't."

Nora wriggled sideways in the passenger seat to glance back. "How could you be sure, Babs? The man is weak. He'd do a lot to win you over. I hope you're not..." The forthright Mrs. Norton didn't finish.

"In love with Tyler? Really, Nora. You should know me better than that. For God's sake, he's Raymond's age." Back in the mirror now, Babette looked offended. "Tyler is pleasant company when he's not being silly. Spitz and I will be quite happy at the farm without a man in our life. Except for family, of course."

The Pom took this as an invitation to clamber onto Babette's lap and to lick her face. For a moment, Louise saw nothing but white fur in the central mirror.

Echoing Louise's earlier thought, Nora remarked, "Antonio might yet haunt him from the grave. That will wouldn't have survived another day if he'd lived. Sorry, dear, to speak of it," she said, glancing at the rear.

Louise slowed at a junction and turned her head to check the road was clear. Shadow wedged his cold snout between the headrest and the doorframe to sneak in a quick lick of her ear. It made Louise smile. How she would have loved an afternoon stroll with the pooch along the gorgeous, tree-lined lanes in their golden fall finery.

"It's okay," Babette said. "Leaving it to Tyler didn't kill him. Talking about a trust fund did."

She sighed. "I still can't wrap my mind around his having a daughter. Lilly, of all people. He was always so mean to her. But to kill her own father? She must have gone insane."

"I doubt it," said Louise. "Warped by hatred and jealousy--yes. Insane--no. Lilly knew what she was doing. I'm afraid she'd reached a point where hearing Tyler being the heir already pushed her over the edge."

"You think so?" Nora sounded skeptical. Then she nodded. "Maybe you are right. The venom that woman spouted after Raymond brought her down from the tower. Terrifying! And to think, Babs, you lived with her day in, day out. Enough to give me nightmares."

"She has her own apartment in the city. I wouldn't have anyone live-in at the condo," Babette said. Then, pensively, "It's frightening to think how she felt about us, how unhappy she was. I should have sensed it and helped her."

"You?" Nora tugged at her seatbelt to swivel toward the rear. "Oh, Babs. Count your lucky stars that the woman wasn't a poisoner and hedged her plans for years."

"Really, Nora. I think you misjudge her," Babette said.

Keeping her eyes on the road, Louise reminded her, "Remember what Lilly told us before the police arrived last night. If she researched and followed Antonio's life from the moment she found his letter, she must be truly obsessed. She virtually stalked him and then pounced when you were looking to replace your housekeeper."

Louise checked the mirrors and caught the reflection of Babette's sad face. Moved by the woman's compassion, she said, "That doesn't mean I don't feel sorry for Lilly. From the sound of it, she had an awful childhood and adolescence. Deserted by her mother and pushed from one foster home to another, no wonder she grew vengeful." Lawyers would make much of that and all the details of Antonio's life that would come out at Lilly's trial. Louise wouldn't put it past Babette to pay for Lilly's defense.

"That man, Gambit, will add it all to his book," said Nora. "Make sure you talk to the lawyers first thing tomorrow, Babs. Someone must stop him."

Tomorrow might be too late, thought Louise. She hadn't checked news sites this morning but expected to see an exclusive in one of the nationals. Unless Jenkins muzzled him for now. Gambit had left around midnight with the police.

The police took Lilly to the mainland and station for questioning within the hour of Raymond arresting her. Two constables remained to take statements. They'd been there for hours. When the officers finally left with Gambit hitching a boat ride to his car, the rest of them felt too exhausted to hash over the events. This morning, they all helped Babette pack her own things to be sent to her condo.

"Take that road over there, Louise." Babette's voice broke into her musings.

Craggy rock faces lined the ascending road they turned onto. The road had no shoulder but verged on overgrown ditches on both sides, studded with trees that hugged the rock.

As the car approached a sharp curve, Babette leaned forward into the gap between the front seats, pointing to the left. "Over there," she whispered.

"Was there always a guardrail?" asked Louise, slowing the car to a crawl. Her fingers hit the four-way flashers.

"Not back then," said Nora, the genteel voice tremulous. "I fastened the bouquet with a ribbon to that tree."

A massive pine, boughless and crooked in its lower half, clung to the rock wall at its rear. A horrendous obstacle to crash into. Louise shivered, contemplating it.

"We can't pull over here," she said. Other cars wouldn't see them in time. A dangerous spot to linger.

No one spoke as the car now climbed a steep ascent for more than half a mile. Near the top, the vista opened. A lookout sign pointed to a track on their right. Though they'd encountered hardly any traffic on the way up, several vehicles were parked in the visitor lot.

Louise picked a space off to the side and cut the engine. It served as a signal for the dogs to jump up and clamor to be set free. Spitz stood yipping on Babette's lap, causing Nora to fling both hands over her ears. Amazed at Babette's docility, Louise grabbed the leash and dashed out of the car to take control of the excited canines.

The grassy space, surrounded by deciduous trees clad in orange, yellow, and red foliage, invited sightseers to stay at picnic tables. What drew the eye, however, was the unbelievably gorgeous view over rolling farmland down both sides and the magnificent fall splendor descending to the bay hundreds of yards below. Far ahead, the water dazzled blue, shading into grays at the shimmering horizon.

They walked the length of the open area, only to veer toward the center with its bay view. When Nora fished a lacy handkerchief from her pocket and placed it on the picnic table, Babette and Louise took the hint. They sat in a row, facing the panorama. Resigned to human inertia, the dogs crawl under the table for a snooze.

For a few minutes, they sat in silence. Babette's hands interlaced on the weathered tabletop. On Babette's other side, Nora fidgeted, probably impatient to get home. Louise noticed that the widow's ring finger showed white where a wedding band had prevented the skin from tanning. Babette wore no rings at all today.

Aware there was little time before they must leave, and loath to discuss an emotional topic while driving, Louise said, "You didn't ask me why I wanted us to take this detour and probably thought it was ghoulish curiosity."

"Oh, I'd never think that," Babette assured her. "You told me you'd explain later. All these years, I've avoided this beautiful spot and found excuses when our guests asked me to come along. Antonio refused too." She smiled at Nora. "You wouldn't even visit Eagle Roost after...after the accident."

Mrs. Norton patted the widow's folded hands, saying, "We are always so much cozier chatting at Rosewood or at Raymond's with Clara and little Nina."

Curious now, Louise said, "Did Antonio visit, too?"

Nora tittered uneasily. "No. It's always only us."

Louise's gaze fixed on the horizon, where clouds moved in from the northwest. She asked, "Babette, did you skim Gambit's exposé at all?" She'd passed on his writing after breakfast this morning before packing her belongings.

"Sorry, no. I stuffed it into my bag. I'll get to it in a day or two."

"That's okay. I assumed you'll wait until you got home, but just wanted to forewarn you. The tone of his writing is often vindictive. We now know it's personal. What disturbs me is that he hints at something fishy about the fatal accident of Raymond's parents. Gambit insinuates it was too opportune and profitable for Antonio."

Babette's sharp intake of breath warned her to exert caution.

Nora winced and sat bolt upright. As if to herself, she said, "How could he know anything? Hank and I always wondered."

"So did I," murmured Babette.

"You?" Nora's cry disturbed the dogs. Shadow bonked his head, sitting up so suddenly under the table. Spitz's black button nose pushed upward between Babette and Louise. The Pom's paws danced up a moment later, begging for room on the bench. Louise slid aside, and Babette lifted Spitz onto her lap.

Once the dogs quieted down, Nora said, "I don't

understand, Babs. You never even hinted at anything sinister back then or since."

"How could I?" Babette's chin leaned on Spitz's head. Her words, muffled, were a mere whisper. "He was my husband. I was too young and frightened."

Calculating rapidly, Louise figured Babette must have been in her early 30s. Still, a husband tough as Arcadia and 20 years her senior probably intimidated the young wife.

Cautious not to spook Babette by showing too much interest, Louise said, "Just an uneasy feeling? Or was it more concrete?"

The widow's hands tensed and buried deeper into Spitz's fluffy, white coat. "How could I be sure?" Her hands shook, then clenched so hard the Pom wriggled from her grip and scrabbled over onto Louise's safer lap.

Nora stroked Babette's hand. "Don't upset yourself, dear. Maybe you'll feel better if you tell us. Shared sorrow eases the mind."

Babette leaned forward, her eyes even bluer in reflecting the azure sky. Her hands clasped each other tightly. In a strangely monotonous voice, she spoke.

"It was just us and Franco and Natalie that weekend. Antonio and Franco were in a bad mood. We heard them arguing the night before. On Sunday morning, Antonio took the boat to get something on the mainland. He wouldn't take me along. When he got back after lunch, he joked and laughed and said we should all go for dinner that night."

Babette glanced at Nora, saying, "You know how much fun he could be when things were going right for him."

"Oh, yes," agreed Mrs. Norton.

But a sideways glance at the serious face told Louise her friend disapproved of Antonio's idea of fun.

"So, did you go for dinner together that night?" Louise asked. She wondered how Franco and Natalie could have ended up on that lonely road.

"No, we didn't. Somehow, the guys had decided in the afternoon that we should first go up to this lookout to see the full moon. We'd done it the year before one evening, and it was really lovely having a champagne picnic up here. When we got to the dock on the mainland, Franco saw his car had a flat tire. Antonio gave him the keys to the old Jimmy we kept up here and insisted he and I follow in his Mercedes. That was rather odd..." She petered off as if lost in thought.

Softly, Louise prompted, "Why was it strange?"

Babette's head turned to gaze at her. "You see, the keys to the Jimmy were on a hook in the kitchen at Eagle Roost. We never carried a spare with us. Usually, we all went in one car when going somewhere on the mainland."

"Did you ask your husband about it?" Louise said.

The widow's brief laugh didn't sound amused. "You don't know my husband. No one questioned his whims. Franco often grumbled but went along with Tony's ideas." She shook her head as though it now seemed unbelievable to her.

"Younger brothers often do," said Nora. "Franco always seemed far younger than the two-year age difference warranted."

"Was that the only strange thing that happened that night?" Louise asked.

"When saying it out loud, it doesn't sound like anything to wonder about," Babette said thoughtfully. "There was more. It was dark and windy when we got here. We drank champagne. I remember the moon hiding behind clouds that raced overhead. I felt chilly. Natalie had a blanket we kept in the Jimmy, and we huddled under it. She was just telling me a funny story about Raymond when Tony said we would be late for our dinner reservations. I said I would drive with Natalie and Franco to the restaurant. My husband grabbed my arm and wouldn't let me get into the SUV." She rubbed her left arm as if needing to soothe it.

"Which of you drove ahead?" Louise asked, fearing she knew the answer.

"When we were in the Mercedes, Tony honked and opened his window. He shouted to Franco, 'Race you to the bottom.' Franco shot off so fast, the gravel spit from under his tires. My husband waited until he was well ahead before following along the gravel drive to the paved road. We saw the Jimmy's rear lights already halfway down. Franco was speeding. Tony didn't even try to catch up. I thought he was going extra slow."

She stopped abruptly and covered her face with her palms.

Nora slung an arm around Babette's shaking back. Spitz pushed her doggy snout against Babette's ribs, whimpering softly. Louise stroked the Pom's back.

"I'm sorry," murmured Babette. "It haunts my dreams. I'll see it happen to the end of my life."

"It might not come back, now that you've talked about it. I'm so very sorry you carried it alone all these years," Nora said. "I only wish you had told me and Hank."

"How could I? You were his friends. And you had Raymond to think of." To Louise, she said, "What was there to tell, anyway? It was all in my head. I was ill for weeks. Later, I convinced myself I was imagining things."

On Babette's other side, Nora muttered, "Tony had the know-how."

Startled, both Louise and Babette leaned forward to stare at the older woman.

"What do you mean, Nora?" Louise asked, and the widow echoed her.

"Don't you know, Babs? When Franco and Tony were young, they fixed their own cars. Tony was much better at it and did all the mechanical work for their restaurants early on. That's what made me wonder back then. Hank wouldn't hear of it."

"I didn't." Babette's voice was colorless. "When I married him, he never fixed things himself."

"Didn't the coroner order an investigation?" Louise asked.

"The coroner back then was a friend of my husband. They golfed and went boating together whenever we were up here."

Though Babette spoke without emphasis, the implications came through clearly. No reason to assume the coroner was covering up a crime, Louise figured. Likely, he wanted to spare the grieving brother the agony and indignity of an investigation. If it looked like a mechanical brake failure in an old vehicle that was infrequently used, why waste police resources and taxpayers' money on forensics? Or so the coroner might have argued.

For all they knew, it might have been just that. A tragic accident, due to misfortune. No matter how financially advantageous for the surviving brother.

Louise remembered Jenkins's tone when she overheard him mentioning the accident. In all the years, he never forgot it. A sign it hadn't seemed straightforward to him. Antonio had gone alone to the mainland earlier that day. Ample time to give Franco's car a flat and fiddle with the Jimmy's brakes on the isolated dock.

Kill his own brother? Horrific. Though the vicar, she thought, would quote a precedent case.

 With a deep sigh, she rose to leave. Some mysteries remain unsolved. If fratricide was done, divine justice caught up with Antonio Arcadia in the end.

Book Club Questions For Death at Eagle Roost

Whether you're reading on your own, with friends, or in your book club, these questions are designed to spark reflection and conversation about Death at Eagle Roost.

1. What roles do animals and domestic routines play in grounding the story?
2. Who are your favorite characters? What do you love or love to hate about them?
3. Which character's choices feel most understandable to you—even if you disagree?
4. Which relationship dynamics feel most intriguing?

5. When do you find yourself trusting a character's account—and when not?

6. Sgt. Raymond Marpel is caught between family loyalty and his RCMP training. Did you sympathize with his position? Should he have acted differently?

7. Secrets--both long-kept and recently revealed—drive the mystery. Which secret struck you as the most pivotal, unexpected, or shocking?

8. The Eagle Roost summer residence is a closed setting filled with tension. How did the house and landscape shape your reading experience? Is there any symbolism in the setting of this mystery?

9. The story unfolds over Thanksgiving weekend, a holiday that often emphasizes gratitude and family unity. How does this contrast with the fractured relationships?

10. Were there moments when you thought you had solved the mystery—only to be misled? Which twists surprised you the most?

11. What turned out to matter more than you expected—and what mattered less?

12. Which themes rose to the surface for you or resonated most?
13. Did you feel justice was reached at the end? Why, and in what way? Or, why not?

Bonus Questions for Louise Penfold Mystery Specialists

i. Louise is again drawn into detecting, but this time within the tense setting of a family gathering. Did you see her role and challenges here as different from *Death at Rosewood Manor*?
ii. Nora acts as Louise's partner in sleuthing—how does their dynamic evolve in this book?
iii. Did your view of Sgt. Marpel change over the course of Book 2?
iv. How did this installment evolve the series' world and relationships?

Catch up on Death at Rosewood
Manor – Louise Penfold Mystery –
Book 1 @
amazon.com/dp/B0DJ3PTPRN

Dear Reader

It's a wonderful feeling to be part of a community of readers and mystery lovers. As story ideas germinate in my mind, and the characters walk in, I get so excited about sharing them with you. When you like my mysteries, it makes my day!

Thank you so much for reading my books!

Warmest regards,

Eva

P.S. As a special favor to support my One Woman Self-publishing enterprise, please be so kind to leave a little review of *Death at Eagle Roost* on Amazon.

Thank You!

Acknowledgments

As always author Rebecca Markus, made time in her busy life to provide helpful feedback. I'm truly privileged to have such a wonderful critique partner. (And it's a great pleasure to read her books, too:) Thanks so much, Rebecca!

My beta reader, Naomi, commented thoroughly on the opening chapters (and would have read the draft if my publication timing had allowed for it). I greatly appreciate her input. Thanks, Naomi. You'll get to read the finished mystery:)

Big thanks go to my awesome editor, Pam Clinton, who was incredibly prompt in proofreading the manuscript. She has the last word about pesky commas and sneaky autocorrects. But any remaining errors and idiosyncrasies rest on my writerly shoulders.

With a heavy heart, I give tribute to my most faithful writing companion. My beloved dog passed peacefully after a long life of loyal friendship. This book is dedicated to Nina, the best dog in the world.

Agnes Taylor Mysteries by Eva Bernhard

Read with Ease Whodunits

Large Print paperback and hardcover editions

Large Print – Agnes Taylor Mysteries

amazon.com/dp/B0D8K71ZMM

Large Print editions make wonderful gifts for yourself, friends, and loved ones 🤍

Also in eBook and standard print editions

Agnes Taylor Mystery series

amazon.com/dp/B099436TY2

Find my books and follow me on me for New Release Alerts

amazon.com/author/evabernhard

and on bookbub.com/authors/eva-bernhard